Keep the Baby, Faith

By Philip DeGrave

KEEP THE BABY, FAITH
UNHOLY MOSES

Keep the Baby, Faith

PHILIP DEGRAVE

PUBLISHED FOR THE CRIME CLUB BY
DOUBLEDAY & COMPANY, INC.
GARDEN CITY, NEW YORK
1986

Library of Congress Cataloging-in-Publication Data

DeGrave, Philip.
Keep the baby, Faith.

I. Title.
PS3554.E416K4   1986   813′.54   86–2127
ISBN 0-385-19742-X

For Carol Brener

Keep the Baby, Faith

Prologue

She had to look at the listing three times before she could believe her eyes, but there it was—Ross, H. L., and the address. On East Seventy-ninth, for God's sake. The last time she'd seen Harry Ross, he'd been living with his parents in Scarsdale, New York, just out of college and talking about going to New York to live, to find a job, to set New York journalism on its ear.

Faith didn't know about the rest of the agenda (three years was little enough time to become famous in, she supposed), but the brother of her best friend from high school had certainly moved to New York, to one of the classiest neighborhoods in Manhattan, high rises and singles bars, jogging in Carl Schurz Park. It was illegal to refer to it in print as anything but "New York's posh Upper East Side."

"You all right, honey?"

Faith started, tensed her muscles, got ready to run. This was a mistake, she should know better by now than to try to move quickly with her hand in the shape it was. Faith wouldn't have thought that her thumb, of all things, could be affected by a simple movement of her head, but it was. Turning her head too fast caused her left hand to punish her, sending her brain pain signals that made the dull ache she felt the rest of the time seem pleasant by comparison. Carefully, Faith put her hand under her coat, resting it on top of her belly, soothing the pain under the warmth of her breast. She couldn't have run anymore to save her life. To save any life.

It was an infinite relief to realize she didn't need to. The speaker was the counterman, the only other human being in the yellow-vinyl all-night diner she'd ducked into to catch her breath. He was a large, head-shaven black man whose figure bulged nearly as much as her own. His face was kind; so was his voice. He wasn't out to get her. There were millions of people in this city, and hardly any of them were out to get her. She had to remember that. Had to *believe* it.

Faith forced herself to smile. "Yes. I'm fine. Thank you."

He looked at her torn coat, the scrape on her forehead. "What happened?" he asked. "Did you fall down?"

Faith remembered the car, the headlights sweeping like scythes across the pavement, remembered realizing that it wasn't going to stop, that it was coming *after her*, and it wasn't going to stop. She remembered the split second of paralysis, then the wild dive for the pavement, thinking as she fell, *the baby, mustn't land on the baby.* She remembered throwing her arms out to catch herself, feeling the click in her hand as the thumb bent the wrong way under her weight.

"Yes," she said. "I fell down."

"Lady in your condition ought to be more careful," he said. "Not a good idea to be out so late, either."

"Yes," Faith said.

"Look, there's a washroom, if you want to freshen up or something. Just behind the counter here. It ain't fancy, but it's clean."

"No," Faith said. "Thank you." She remembered to smile. "I just needed to look up this phone number."

She *hadn't* needed to look up the phone number. She *had* the phone number. It was the phone number that told her the Seventy-ninth Street address was the Harry Ross she knew and no other.

She pushed the phone book back across the counter with her good hand. "Thanks."

"Think nothing of it," the counterman told her. "You want a cup of coffee or something? On the house."

"No," Faith said. "Nothing. Thank you." Faith had to get away. The man was being nothing but nice, but a woman, a *pregnant* woman, who has just survived the fourth attempt on her life in as many days is not ready to deal with nice.

Faith took her injured hand out of the warmth, got off the stool, and left before the counterman could offer her some other unwanted kindness.

Outside, she took a lungful of cold night air, oriented herself, and set off. She walked slowly, to keep from jarring her hand, and she stayed close to the buildings. Under ordinary circumstances, that wasn't wise—muggers liked to wait in doorways, and reach out and grab women who walked close to buildings—but tonight, Faith was more afraid of the car than she was of any mugger.

And, it seemed, the muggers had all stayed home tonight. Too cold, perhaps. Faith had too much else to think about to worry about it. She kept making slow, steady progress south. Toward Harry. Tonight, Faith needed a friend.

CHAPTER ONE

It's not like me to say this, but I really don't have any right to complain about what happened. The night Faith stumbled (literally) into my life, I was *hoping* for something to happen. Something different. Something exciting. That will teach me.

My name is Harry Ross. A good Scottish name. However. That's "Harry" as in Harry, not as in Henry V, for example. And it's "Ross" not as in "clan of," but as in Rosenzweig. My father would have been just as good a dentist if he'd had his diploma issued to Dr. Rosenzweig, and would have made my mother just as much money to spend in Bloomingdale's. He might even have gotten into the country club, especially in Scarsdale, but you would never have been able to convince him of that. He's dead now. An internist who'd changed his name to Buckingham was treating him for ulcers, and he died of stomach cancer. My mother still lives in Scarsdale (the house is paid for), and still spends money at Bloomie's. My sister lives with her, when she's home from Syracuse. I have the normal complement of aunts and uncles and even cousins, all named Ross. (Grandma Rosenzweig gave up a couple of years ago, bitter at not having enough money in her own name to make it worthwhile to make a will to leave people out of.) There are doctors and lawyers and accountants. There are college professors. There is even a fantastically successful choreographer, my cousin Eliot. He's gay as Mardi Gras, and his mother actually once stuck her head in the oven over it, but eventually, Aunt Bertha faced the inevitable, and has taken to bragging about "my son, the fantastically successful choreographer." The Rosses (or whatever) have done really well for a family just three generations in the States.

But they *all* brag about me. My son/nephew/cousin the journalist. They actually say journalist. I work for The Grayness. Every journalist in the world wants to work for The Grayness. And why not? The Grayness is probably the Greatest Publication There Absolutely Ever Was, the World's Diary. If The Grayness hasn't reported it, it doesn't exist. No. That's not exactly right. If The Grayness hasn't reported it, you are a Better Person for not knowing it. The Grayness is printed on cheap paper with cheaper ink (it's the only way many New Yorkers ever soil their hands), but its influence can topple governments; earn the authors of plays and books millions of dollars.

So everybody wants to work for The Grayness. Journalism students send padded resumes to the unassuming building off the square. Working reporters at lesser papers (i.e., any paper that isn't The Grayness) dream of breaking a Big Story, and being invited to join the National Affairs Staff. Deep Thinkers at Famous Liberal Universities eagerly await the call to write Learned Articles for the op-ed page. Authorities in various fields hope to be given the opportunity by the Book Review to assassinate books written by their rivals.

Everybody wants to work for The Grayness, especially the ones who already do. Except me. I'd been on vacation for two weeks, now, with one week to go, and I was looking forward to going back the way I'd look forward to a course of root-canal work.

The cachet, the unadulterated odor of sanctity about that paper, is amazing. People I don't even know seem especially impressed. I can almost see them thinking, My God, the kid's not thirty yet, and he works for (pause) The Grayness. If I run into any doubters, I have a press card to prove it. And if I manage to get away from them before they ask the inevitable next question, I sometimes even leave them impressed.

God knew I sure wasn't. Yeah (my editor at The Grayness would change this to "yes"), I was one of the Fortunate Few deemed worthy to work for the Greatest Publication, etc. I did the TV listings, and I was going nuts.

I mean, my God, every day, lists of numbers and one-sentence write-ups of network and local shows. Check out any questions with the stations, where someone my age, going just as wacko, was standing by for just such an eventuality.

It's hard to say what the worst thing about such a job is. One of the worst things is not being able to *complain* to anybody about it. At The Grayness, people will avoid like the proverbial dead skunk anyone who isn't a "real reporter." Outside, people can't get over what an easy job it is I've got, all the prestige of The Grayness, but Monday to Friday, nine to five, with no necessity of going anywhere you'd have to duck PLO bullets in search of a story.

And great pay, too, enough to allow me to rent a two-bedroom apartment in a high rise at Seventy-ninth and York. Ask the nearest New Yorker what kind of money that takes these days. The job pays a lot of money because, although it is boring shitwork of the first magnitude, it is important. One of the major lies The Grayness tells itself is that its readers are Too Intelligent To Watch Television—Except Perhaps Wimbledon, And Occasionally PBS. Fortunately for The Grayness, the powers that be are smart enough to know when a cherished lie can cost them money. If the person doing the listings ever misplaced the "A-Team" or the "Odd Couple" reruns on Channel 11, The Grayness's circulation would drop like a rock, and all those refeened secret closet TV-watchers would get their listings from *New York* magazine. They would die rather than be caught buying *TV Guide.* I don't tell you this to brag; it's an important part of what happened later.

I hated my job; I loved my apartment. I had my furniture, and five thousand books, mostly mysteries, humor, and science fiction. I had a twenty-four-inch Sony color TV, and two VCRs, and a stereo and records and tapes. I should have been happy, and I would have been—if only I could stand what I was doing for a living.

It might have helped, if, after having me write every conceivable type of news story, a body of work equal in length to *War and Peace*, before hiring me, The Grayness actually let me write something for publication every once in a while. But probably not. There is only so much you can write about the latest BBC story of Incredibly Sensitive Upper Class English People In The Years Before World War I that is running on PBS (the Primarily British System), made possible by a grahnt from Mobil (better make that the Petroleum Broadcasting Service). These shows are the only thing The Grayness will admit its readers watch on television. Give me "Miami Vice" any day.

Not that I have anything against British TV, mind you. Or PBS, either. That very night, I watched three different actors play "Doctor Who" on three different area PBS stations (I love cable). That's what I should have been, I thought. Not an actor —I should have been Doctor Who. Or possibly Indiana Jones.

My problem was, I was too romantic. Always had been. Got my ideas of journalism from old Pat O'Brien movies, and never let go of them until mental gangrene started to set in at The Grayness.

I sighed. I reflected, not for the first time, that the best thing for depression would be some Great Sex. Or even Borderline Acceptable Sex. A Peck On The Cheek would even be nice. It had been a long time. My previous girlfriend (two years' worth, mind you) had led me to a remarkable discovery. Women in New York do not want to know men who are depressed. Especially men who are depressed about their jobs. They want to know men who are stockbrokers who make a hundred and sixty-seven thousand dollars a year and up, and who love every second of their fast-paced, high-pressure lives. It also helps if he is six feet tall and looks like Robert Redford.

I am six feet tall.

Where was I? Oh, right, depressed. I should have known. Women in New York also do not like to be with men who are depressed, because that reduces the amount of time they can spend thinking about how depressed *they* are. The women are depressed because All The Men In New York Are Either Married Or Gay.

This is an irrefutable fact. The poor schmucks who sit at home Friday nights, wishing they were some character in a movie, and trying to forget the six nearly memorized issues of *Pent-*

house sitting secretly on a high shelf in a closet, do not exist. They are figments of their own imagination.

My God, how did I get started on this? Excuse it, please.

Anyway, Great Sex being unavailable, I decided to do what I usually did, and drown my sorrows in an anchovy pizza. I could have called and had it delivered, but the doorman got paranoid over late-night deliveries, and I wanted to get some fresh air. Cold air, at least. In New York, you don't ask for fresh. I slipped into a pair of Ponys, and headed up to York Avenue Pizza.

I did my New York drill as I walked home, balancing the pizza on one hand, while I kept the other in my pocket, grasping my keys. This not only reduced the time it would take to get inside my apartment (in case someone followed me up the elevator), it gave me an instant weapon, like a set of brass knuckles with teeth, to be raked across the face of the pack of drug-crazed juvenile delinquents who were roaming the streets of Yorkville, each carrying a switchblade with my name on it.

Nobody bothered me. Nobody ever bothered me. Part of it was probably the neighborhood. Yorkville is the last of the middle-class family neighborhoods in Manhattan, and muggings are thin on the ground compared to some areas. People still get nervous—people in New York are always nervous about something. Some carry pistols on the subway, and even shoot them, but I go my way, always taking precautions, never needing them. That's probably better than the other way around.

Somebody was arguing with the doorman when I got there. "I have to see him," she said. "I *have* to!"

"He's no home," Ramon, the doorman, told her. He speaks much better English than that, he just gets tired of dealing with Broadway groupies and movie groupies and literary groupies and various other kinds of maniacs who lay siege to the mid-level celebrities who live in the building. He figures people give up arguing sooner with someone who can barely understand them. "He's no home," Ramon said again. "I see him go out. You come back tomorrow." I smiled. Tomorrow, the day man would be on.

Anyway, Ramon seemed to have the situation in hand, so I figured it was safe to approach the doorway.

That's when the woman screamed my name, and rushed out of the doorway at me.

CHAPTER TWO

My first thought was don't drop the pizza. I knew it was idiotic the moment it came to me. But I didn't drop the pizza, either. I did pull my right hand from my pocket, holding tight to my keys.

I wanted to stop and figure out what this woman wanted with me—I mean, it's ridiculous. There *are* no TV listings groupies.

That, I decided, would have to wait for a better time. The obvious next step was to figure out how to use the keys to any effect if I was so determined to hold on to the pie. Fortunately, I didn't have to work that one out. Not only was the intruder a woman, she was a pregnant woman. She was so slow and so stiff, she was no threat to anybody.

Besides, she was more frightened than I could ever be. If I were carrying a naked machete instead of a pizza, she couldn't have been more afraid. It didn't seem to be me she was so scared of, it was more like she was living with a level of fear the way a person with gout lives with a level of pain. My sudden belligerence was like someone stepping on a gouty foot. She jumped, blanched, and let out a hopeless little scream. She froze, even stopped breathing.

Then I looked at her face. I couldn't believe it. "Faith?" I said.

The woman let her breath go. "Harry," she said. "Thank God."

"Let me get this straight," I said half an hour later. "You called my mother in Scarsdale to find out where I was, but she wouldn't tell you."

"That's right." Faith looked a little better now. She'd spent most of the half hour in the bathroom moaning and running cold water over her swollen left hand. I had managed to get her face washed, and to put Mercurochrome and a Band-Aid on her forehead.

"Why not?" I demanded. It seemed to me my mother would be more likely to volunteer to come to the city and personally escort a girl to my door. Especially Faith Sidon, my sister's best friend from high school.

"She gave me your phone number. Said you were in Manhattan."

"Where were you?"

"Midtown. I was at a hotel, but I couldn't stay there anymore."

"How long have you been in New York?"

"A week. Six days."

"You should have come to me to begin with, dope." That was inadvertent. Older brothers always refer to high-school-age sisters and their friends as "dope." Faith had obviously been through a few changes since I'd seen her last (about three and a half years ago), but I was falling immediately into the old habit. I resolved to watch myself.

Faith didn't even notice. "It wouldn't have been fair," she said. "It still isn't. You have no idea what I might be letting you in for. If I had anywhere else to go, I would. I even thought of taking the train to Scarsdale and calling on your mother, but when she wouldn't give me your address, I got all paranoid. I've been paranoid a lot, lately."

I said, "Even paranoids have enemies," but Faith didn't laugh. "What I don't understand, is why my mother put you off."

"She got paranoid, too. Didn't believe I was me. I think my big mistake was asking for Sue."

Sue is my sister. She's majoring in petroleum chemistry at Syracuse University, which is a big shock for a girl who spent her childhood trying to decide whether to be Sylvia Plath, and commit poetic suicide, or to take the world of ballet by storm. I'm going to go on spelling it "Sue." My sister changes. First, she made it "Su," which probably influenced her choice of college.

Then she decided there might be other Susans out there spelling it that way, so she decided on "Soo." That, however, wasn't dignified enough for a potential Nobel Prize winner, so lately, she's been trying "Sioux." It might help her get a job, if somebody has a minority-hiring policy.

"She's at school at the moment, though she should be home for Thanksgiving pretty soon."

Faith nodded, then winced. She held her hand up against her shoulder. I figured I ought to go rig up a sling for her or something.

She wanted to talk. "Tomorrow. Your mother told me that much. Then I asked where I could find you—I figured I was in Manhattan, and the last I'd heard you were just about to move to Manhattan, and I really needed to see a friendly face, you know?"

"Sure," I said. "I'm glad you did."

"Well, your mother apparently thought this was some kind of scam, I was fronting for some white slave ring or something, out to get Sue. Maybe she figured the gang would kidnap you and hold you for a swap or something. Your mother said it was nothing personal, but she didn't like your being in New York, and didn't trust people looking for you there. So she gave me your phone number and said she'd leave it up to you. She said since they hadn't heard from me in three years—"

"Who has? Two weeks after graduation you ran off to Europe, and nobody has seen you since. Sue talks about you all the time. She wouldn't admit it, but I think you kind of hurt her."

"You know why, Harry. I'd just turned eighteen, I got hold of that thirty thousand dollars my father left me, and I'd had just about enough of Scarsdale. I took the money and ran."

"I know," I said. "Sue showed me your postcard. Hell, with thirty thousand bucks and an income—you had an income, right? With that kind of money you could have phoned."

"Things happened."

For the first time, I looked significantly at Faith's stomach. "I can see that."

"I'm married. This is a legitimate baby. This is a *special* baby.

It's the only baby I'll ever have. It's Paul's baby." She said it the way the Virgin Mary might have said, "it's God's baby."

Under normal circumstances, I would have been all over Faith with questions about this Paul character. Like, where the hell was he when his pregnant wife was wandering around New York late at night, accosting doormen, scaring pizza-laden old friends to death. With every second that went by, though, I could see the circumstances were getting farther and farther from normal. All right, Faith had been my sister's best friend, almost like another kid sister to me, but I hadn't seen her in over three years. A lot could happen in three years. Apparently, a lot *had* happened in three years.

Faith was sitting in the straight-back chair in the corner of the room, near the front door, with her head thrown over the back of the chair in utter weariness. There was a perfectly comfortable overstuffed armchair in front of the window, but Faith was having none of it. She liked to sit with her back to the wall, she said. Now she had her right arm across her stomach, and her left elbow planted on the arm of the chair, with her forearm straight up, supporting her injured hand like an unwanted burden.

I could see that she had really wracked it up. The thumb was the worst, huge and discolored the way it was, but her whole hand was swollen. I hadn't noticed the wedding ring before because the gold band had nearly been swallowed in flesh. It was, I must admit, a test of macho to look at.

"You must be hungry," I said. It was all I could think of. "Do you want some pizza? I could pop a slice into the microwave and heat it up."

"God, no," Faith said. "I couldn't keep it down. I haven't been able to keep anything in my stomach for days."

"You'd better eat something." Somewhere in Scarsdale, Helen Ross was smiling.

Faith was smiling, too, leaning back in the chair with her eyes closed. "My father used to talk like that."

"I'll feed you something when we get back from the hospital," I said.

Faith's eyes came open. "Hospital?"

"Yes, hospital. We're going to have that hand looked at. We're going to make sure you're okay. We're going to make sure the baby is okay."

"The baby is fine," Faith said. "Thank God. I can feel him kicking."

"He's kicking you because you haven't fed him in three days. And you are going to the hospital. Right now. It's great to see you again and all, but I'll be damned if I'm going to sit here and watch you put creases in your face trying not to wince."

"I—I'll be all right."

"You'll be all right because you're getting medical attention."

"Harry, no!"

"Faith, don't be ridiculous—"

"It's dangerous."

"There's no boogeyman out there, just muggers. Which we will avoid by taking a cab. Are you ashamed or something? Because you fell down? It's pretty silly if you are. I mean, everybody takes a bad fall every once in a while."

Faith sprang to her feet. Her brown eyes were blazing, the damaged hand forgotten. "I didn't fall! I jumped! They're after the baby! They're trying to *kill Paul's baby!*" Then the fire in the eyes went out. She swayed and collapsed. I sprang from the sofa and got to her just in time to catch her before she crashed baby-first onto my fancy sealed-wood floor.

CHAPTER THREE

I was sitting on a slippery plastic chair not-looking at a black and white movie on a TV set mounted out of reach high above the doorway to the emergency room. With an impartiality commendable in a journalist, I was also not-looking at a worn and ancient copy of *Newsweek*, thereby avoiding a rehearsal of the details of another crisis that had somehow failed to destroy us. These crises are always going to destroy us. You'd think no journalist (or better yet, no reader they aim this stuff at) had ever heard of World War II. If the German and Japanese didn't destroy us with their armies, I doubt they'll be able to do it with a few million compact cars.

Even if I harbored those kinds of fears, I wouldn't have been worried about them, then. I was too busy wondering what I was getting into. I was raised to know you should always be ready to help a friend, even a sister's friend. But all this was a little strange.

It was inevitable, I supposed, that Sue's best friend would turn out to be somebody like Faith. In appearance, they were a good example of what I like to call the Betty-and-Veronica syndrome. Same height, and they'd be about the same weight if Faith weren't pregnant. The differences were all superficial, designed to make it easier to tell them apart in a newspaper comic section. Sue had curly blond hair, round blue eyes, and glasses. Faith's hair was straight and brown. She had brown sloe eyes, no glasses. Sue was bubbly, full of ideas, good and otherwise, as her constant name changes demonstrate. Faith had always been reserved. I couldn't remember now if by reserved I meant serene, or eerily quiet. The evidence tonight was all for the latter, though that could be a reaction to the injury, or silent

rebuke of me for hauling her off to the hospital in spite of
protests (delivered while she was still woozy from her faint) that
she was fine, really, don't go to all this fuss.

They kept her in there a long time. I was just about to go find
out if she'd skipped out on me when she rejoined me. They'd
done a job on her thumb—you would have thought she'd fractured her arm or something. There was a splint, an Ace bandage
running halfway up her arm, and a sling.

"Feeling better?" I asked.

Faith showed me a shy smile. "Lots. They did a good job. I'm
glad you brought me here, after I made such a fuss. You've been
very kind," she said.

"You act like you're surprised. Who was always driving you
and Sue around town to shop? Who loaned you two money, and
didn't make a snotty remark when it got paid back?"

"I didn't mean that, Harry. Sue will kill me for telling you this,
but she always used to say how lucky she was to have you for a
brother, considering what idiots most boys were."

"That sounds like her."

"And I used to have a crush on you myself."

I looked to heaven. "If I'd only *known!*"

"Oh, I knew nothing could come of it. I mean, you were three
years older than we were, and you were going out with Helen
Wasser . . ."

Helen Wasser. My girlfriend all through high school. We spent
the week before we went away to our various colleges losing—
hell, *squandering* our respective virginities. Once we'd done
that, we realized that our relationship had been based on the
tension of the delay, and we drifted apart. By second term, we
weren't even writing to each other anymore.

"Well," I said. "I'm glad I—or at least my family—was what
you thought of when you got ready to make a return appearance. And now you're going to come back to my place—"

"Could I?" she said. Her voice held a mixture of equal parts
gratitude and relief. "Thanks, Harry. I wouldn't put you
through this, but I don't have anywhere to go."

"You can tell me all about who's trying to get you."

Faith said, "No. That's impossible."

I shrugged. I was so casual, I amazed myself, especially since I knew I would eat a live caterpillar to learn Faith's story. A lot of it was vulgar curiosity (who would want to kill a nice Catholic girl from Scarsdale?), but a lot of it was also a determination to find out if Faith was nuts before I let my sister rush to her side, as she undoubtedly would as soon as she got home from school tomorrow.

"If you don't trust me . . ."

"It's not that," she protested. "If I didn't trust you, I wouldn't have asked you to help."

"Then there's no problem," I said. I smiled, and somehow failed to see the look of chagrin on Faith's face.

We went outside into the cold damp air, and headed west to York Avenue to get a cab.

Faith said, "Oh!"

"What's the matter?"

"I just realized what you must be thinking."

"I'm not thinking anything, I'm just curious."

"You haven't said a word about my being pregnant. And I told you I'm in trouble . . ." She blushed. "Well, I am, but not that kind of trouble. It's much worse than anything like *that*. I mean, I'm married. Really. I have been for two years. That's not the problem. Well, actually, I guess it is. But it's not a problem with the baby. It's my husband's baby. There's no legitimacy question or anything. It's just that—"

So much for eerily quiet. Now it was nonstop talking, with no real information imparted. She'd told me all this already. I stepped to the curb to hail a taxi. I let a couple go by—with the size Faith was, we needed a Checker. New York would eventually be sorry the company had stopped making those things.

Finally, one came by with its light on. I hailed it, then ushered Faith to the curb. She was still a little shaky, and I didn't want her keeling over on a dirty sidewalk.

As I held the door for her, Faith tossed this one over her shoulder: ". . . and you may have heard of my husband. He's been in the papers, though he hates to be. Paul Letron?"

It occurred to me that I might have to take Faith to a different kind of doctor before I was through with her. I'd heard of Paul Letron, all right. The Grayness was full of stuff about the billionaire playboy-turned-recluse and his equally reclusive family, with all sorts of unlikely speculations about why he'd dropped out of sight about three years ago, and scholarly predictions about what his continuing absence from the public eye would do to his company, and to the cosmetics industry in general.

Right, I thought. I was supposed to believe, apparently, that Paul Letron had dropped out of sight in order to marry my sister's best friend from high school. Mmm hmm. Right. He'd dropped Amelia Earhart for her, no doubt.

I got in the cab and closed the door. The partition that separated the driver from the passengers was closed, but it had holes in it. God only knew what the hackie was making of it all.

Especially the part at the end. Faith was still talking. "That's why I need help. It's the family; Robert and Louis and Peter and Lucille and Alma. Especially Alma."

"What about them?" I asked. I was thinking, soft rooms and plastic spoons, no loud noises, and pills to make you feel better, Faith, dear. I tried to make my voice sound as if I were taking all this seriously.

"What can I do?" Faith asked rhetorically. "They've got power, and connections, and right now, they have all the money in the world. It's Paul's money, and they're using it trying to *kill* me."

CHAPTER FOUR

The pizza had been sitting on the kitchen table, congealing, all the time we'd been at the hospital. I no longer needed it to drown my sorrows, but by now, I was ravenous. Thank God for microwave ovens. I put a couple of slices on a paper plate and asked Faith if she wanted something. She tried to refuse, but I was staunch.

Finally, I induced her to try a cold broiled chicken breast. She needed it, despite her protests. She sat at a chrome-and-butcher-block table (from Bloomingdale's, as featured in the Living Section of The Grayness—a housewarming gift from Mom) and munched the chicken as if it were the last of the breed.

"The baby doesn't like anchovies," she explained. "I learned that the hard way. Did you know in Paris they don't slice pizza? In all of France, I guess. They serve it to you on a plate with a knife and fork, and you have to guess where to cut into it."

"You've been to Paris," I said inanely.

Faith showed class. She had every right to tell me, no, I read about it in a book called *Pizza Habits of the World, Volume 6,* but she didn't. All she did was say yes, and add, "I know you were there. Sue used to show me your postcards."

I had been there. Junior year abroad, Paris, then London. I liked London better by a lot. I know that's a minority opinion, but there it is.

Still, there were some things about Paris that were really terrific. I went to the kitchen and started making hot chocolate from scratch. Faith finished her chicken, went to the sofa, and lowered herself with enough care for a space shuttle landing.

"What are you doing?" she asked.

"Preparing to relive my favorite memory of Paris," I told her. Hot chocolate wouldn't go especially well with the anchovies, but what the hell. Also, I wanted to get a little more nourishment into the expectant mother.

It took a while, but Faith waited patiently. Finally, I was done, and I brought her a mug. She took a quiet sip and said this was the best hot chocolate in the world, next to what they served at Aux Deux Magots on the Boulevard Saint Germain in Paris. I won't pretend I wasn't pleased. I explained how I had personally made fortunes for dairy farmers and investors in cocoa futures in attempts to duplicate the flavor, and the rich, almost syrupy consistency of the famous cafe's blend without making the whole mess cloy.

"I hit on this combination about a month ago. I was pretty sure this was it, but it had been so long since I tasted the real thing, I wasn't positive."

Faith took another sip. "No," she said, "you've got it. It would be absolutely perfect, but you just can't get milk here as good as the milk in France." She looked into her cup like a fortune-teller. "Still, I can't tell you what a nice surprise this is. I hadn't expected anything so good until I was able to get back there."

"You expect to go back, then." One of my major assets as a journalist is that I check all statements, seconds after they are made.

"Oh," Faith said. "Of course I'm going back. I have to. As soon as the baby's born. When the baby comes, everything will be all right. I can go back then. I really never should have left, I know, but the baby is more important than anything. As soon as the baby comes, I can go back to Paris." She said it like a litany, rephrasing from time to time. She concluded with, "After all, that's where Paul is. And he needs me too."

Faith hugged the mug to her, maybe for warmth, maybe for memories. She looked at me, and began to tell her story.

CHAPTER FIVE

Graduation day had not been especially happy for Faith. The whole year had been a trial. Her father had died just before Christmas, after a long, messy illness. She had watched him waste away until there was nothing left.

Faith's mother had been dead for years, since before she could remember, and there were no other relatives. Still, there had been a lot of people at the funeral. Her father had been an honest and well-liked businessman, and of course people felt sorry for her for being alone.

My mother (and Sue) wanted her to come live with us, but Faith decided she'd bring us down instead of us bringing her up, and spent the remainder of the school year living with the principal of the high school and his family. They were considerate and understanding, and had only the best of motives. They made her life a misery for six months. If they weren't after her to "put it behind her and start living again," they were telling other people (never Faith; they were too smart to mention this to Faith) that it was really a mercy, the poor man had been sick such a long time.

And then there was the business about where she wanted to go to college. Mr. Gold, the principal, intimated that in light of her situation, admissions departments would be inclined to disregard the inevitable drop-off in her grades over those last two marking periods, so Faith didn't really need to worry about any of the applications she'd filled out back in the fall.

Even Sue, possibly her only friend, had come up with the idea of their going to the same place. Faith loved Sue, she really did, but it was just impossible. She wished people wouldn't ask her to explain.

Anyway, Faith had already decided college was out of the question. There was just no way she was going to put herself in that kind of situation, where *everyone* she met would be bright and nervous, eager to make new friends. Where are you from? Decided on a major? What does your father do?

No. There was no way she was ready to face that question from a hundred, a thousand, kids her age with full sets of parents and homes to go to. She had to get away.

No one could stop her. She'd turned eighteen at the beginning of June, old enough to vote, drink, join the Army, get married, whatever she wanted. She was decidedly old enough to get a passport.

And she had money. There was the insurance money, and the money her father had invested for her. The income was plenty for a girl of simple tastes to live on. She could go to college any time.

But first, Europe. Paris. After years of pain and bedpans, Faith wanted glamour, and excitement, and all the other cliches a well-read Westchester adolescent can pick up about the Queen of Cities. Above all, she wanted something foreign and new. She wanted to drown herself in new stimuli—if she spent her time wondering what the man in the charcuterie was trying to tell her about the *jambon fumé,* she couldn't be wondering if she'd cared enough, done enough, to make her father's going less painful, more dignified.

She would go to Paris. She would learn French (she'd taken Spanish in school). She would talk to people, tourists and natives, when she felt the need, but when the questions led her down painful ways, she would remember an engagement, or she would not have enough of the language. She would find herself an apartment, in a non-touristy area. She would walk boulevards and sit in cafes and go to museums and see landmarks until she was exhausted, and she would come home and go right to sleep. She might have an unpleasant dream or two, but she had unpleasant dreams already.

She might even, she told herself, try to write. She had harbored a desire to write since she was ten; it was a mark of their

friendship that she'd told Sue about it. She and Sue used to do
comic books; Faith would create elaborate swashbuckling ad-
ventures, with plucky heroines "who while not beautiful, had
about them an air of spirit and mischief that drew men to them
as iron filings to a magnet," and resourceful heroes of a hand-
someness limited only by Sue's ability to draw them.

Now, maybe Faith would find out if she could finally admit
her desire to write to a wider circle, maybe even do something
about it. The only thing wrong with that (and the objection used
to make Faith smile—about the only thing that did, lately) was
that Faith hoped to be the kind of writer who'd be original
enough to reject the musty cliché about alienated young Americans Coming To Paris To Write.

She went to Paris, anyway. She learned a lot of things that
weren't clichés—or, a lot of things she hadn't known before, at
least. Like how much it rained. Faith arrived in the middle of
September, and stood in line in the rain outside the tourist office
on the Champs-Elysées, hoping that one of the fashion buyers
that pack the city at that time of year (she hadn't known about
that, either), would drop dead, or go home, or find religion and
enter a convent, or get arrested. Anything that would free up a
hotel room and get her out of the *rain*.

Eventually, she found a hotel to stay in—three hotels, actually, since the vacancies were only available for a day or two at a
time. She got used to showers in the rooms, but toilets down the
hall. She faced the fact that it was impossible for an American to
use a bidet without feeling like a complete idiot. She went out
and explored the city. And fell in love with it. It rained eighteen
of the first twenty-one days Faith stayed in Paris, but she just
bought an umbrella and went out on every one of them.

She bought French bread, French pastry, French peanuts.
She rode the Métro, everywhere. Or she walked the Métro. At
the Charles de Gaulle-Étoile stop, Faith estimated it was possible to walk a mile and a half underground to get from one train
line to another. None of the guidebooks she bought had anything to say about the topic.

She went to museums and shops. She went to Shakespeare &

Co., the successor to the famous bookstore and literary hangout of the great writers of the twenties, Hemingway and the rest. The ones who'd come to Paris to write before it became a cliché. She respected the history, but was disappointed with the place itself, which was musty, badly organized, and more than a little smug. Also, the roof leaked.

Faith found, through a combination of diligence and luck, an apartment in the fifteenth *arrondissement,* in a modern building with an elevator and a friendly young concierge. It cost approximately one third what the equivalent apartment in New York would cost. It was, like practically all the apartments in France, furnished. She settled in, bought a typewriter, and began to write.

Nothing serious, of course, nothing she actually expected (or wanted) to be *published.* Just thoughts, descriptions. Restaurant reviews. Film reviews. She saw a lot of movies in Paris, American movies, in English ("VO" for *version originale),* with French subtitles.

She didn't write any letters. Not to the Golds, not to Sue. She kept telling herself she should, but just thinking of it reminded her of home, and that reminded her of her father, and that made her want to think of something else.

It wasn't that she wanted to be cut off from *America.* Living in Paris, Faith became a better-informed citizen than she ever had been living in the States. She bought the *International Herald Tribune* every day, and read every word. She got the international editions of *Time* and *Newsweek,* and read them cover to cover. Every week, she went to the W. H. Smith bookstore on the Rue de Rivoli, and bought the New York *Times Book Review, People, Sports Illustrated,* and every other American magazine she could get her hands on.

She followed America like a soap opera, clucking her tongue over campaign gaffes, or smiling at the celebrity gossip. She found that there was a peculiar calming, insulating effect to living abroad. The problems that caused ulcers for concerned Americans looked much smaller from a distance. And it was obvious that everybody in France (everyone in Europe, she

later learned) was obsessed with America and things American.
They ate American breakfast cereals (that came with instruc-
tions that said "pour on milk—cold milk is best"). They wore
American blue jeans, and T-shirts from American colleges.
They drove American cars, when they could afford them. They
watched American TV shows—"Dynasty" (and God help us,
Faith thought) was the top-rated show in both England and
France.

Whether they professed to love America or hate it, they
never stopped using it as the standard against which everything
at home was measured, from economic stability to cultural influence. Faith found it hard to worry too much about her country when she was surrounded by people who (a) depended so
much on it; and (b) didn't seem to be too worried themselves.

And she made new friends. North Americans, mostly—she
was learning French rapidly, but not rapidly enough to have the
kind of conversations that could lead to anything. At first, the
friends found her—a Canadian couple she met at the laundro-
mat on the end of her block, the only decent one, they assured
her, in Paris. He was an engineer, and they'd just decided to
take a year off and Do France Before They Were Too Old. They
helped Faith a lot, answered a lot of questions for her. After a
month or so, they went back to Calgary.

As she learned more of what was going on, Faith began to
adopt people the way the Canadian couple had adopted her.
People scratching their heads in front of Métro maps, or sitting
in cafes wondering what *hamburger au chevaux* could be. Mid-
dle-aged people, mostly, or young couples with kids. Most people seemed delighted to hear an American voice, which kind of
made Faith wonder why they'd come to France in the first
place. For her part, Faith got a kick out of playing Old Paris
Hand. It was good for her confidence. It made her feel grown-
up, and that, she guessed, was the real idea behind all of this—
she had run away to grow up.

For that reason, she avoided places like the Bureau de
Change at the American Express office near the Opéra, or the
cafes or fast food joints around the Boulevard Saint Michel,

where the students from the Sorbonne hung out. She didn't want to meet college students; she especially didn't want to meet *American* college students studying abroad. They'd think she was one of them. They'd ask the same questions. They'd want dates, and Faith had had dates before. They'd probably want sex, which Faith had not yet experienced, and frankly did not think she was ready for.

She steered clear of student-aged Americans until just before Christmas, when she took up with Bess.

It was a cold winter, colder than Westchester. There was a fierce, dry wind that burned and chapped your skin, and sometimes it blew small, abrasive snowflakes before it, so that it felt like you were walking through a storm of Ajax. The weather didn't discourage the crowds from their last-minute Christmas shopping, and it didn't deter Faith from exploring.

She preferred, however, to walk at a New York pace, New York being the only big city she'd known before coming to Paris. It was a pace somewhat faster than the Parisians liked— except when they sprinted along the already rapidly moving sidewalks in the Métro, of course. And with current conditions, Faith would be lucky to be able to get moving at all. There was a large, American-style shopping mall across the street from Faith's building, and the sidewalks and a good part of the streets were packed solid with people.

It occurred to her that this freezing afternoon of December 23 would be an ideal time for her to explore the neighborhood around the university. She'd see a *few* students, of course, but the weather would keep people from talking, and all of the Americans would have gone home for the holidays by now.

That same idea had not occurred to Bess Waters of Hillsdale, New Jersey, who was visiting Paris over the holidays with her widowed mother. Bess was looking for American students to meet, or English-speaking people of any kind, or stray dogs, or anybody she could talk to. Her mother, it seemed, as she frequently did on these trips, had Found Romance, and Bess was sort of in the way. Faith first saw Beth feeding a one-legged pigeon in the Place de la Sorbonne. She was telling the pigeon not to be greedy, but the bird wasn't listening.

She sounded so miserable, Faith forgot her various resolves, and went over to talk to her. At that, it wasn't so bad, because aside from what's your name and where are you from and what brings you to Paris, Bess didn't ask any questions. She talked about herself, and never (mercifully) seemed to notice that Faith volunteered no information of her own. Mostly she talked about How Wonderful Her Mother Was, so alive, so fun-loving. And beautiful, really, simply gorgeous, you'd never believe she was as old as she was. She talked about How Close she and her mother were.

She didn't say she hoped her mother choked, but Faith heard it loud and clear between the gushes.

Anyway, Bess invited Faith to spend Christmas with Mother and her. Faith, who'd been dreading Christmas—being alone, remembering her father in an apron, fixing the best turkey stuffing in Scarsdale—was delighted to accept. Also, Bess had something she wanted to do Christmas Eve. Once again, Bess said nothing about one thing depending on the other, but living in a different language had taught Faith to read between the lines.

Bess wanted to go to Midnight Mass at Notre Dame. They'd been here for Christmas three times, and she'd never made it to Notre Dame—never made it to mass at all, actually. By the time Christmas Day rolled around, Mother was usually too tired to be bothered, and it would be such a drag to go by yourself . . .

Faith had no great enthusiasm for the plan, but she agreed. Something else to do, something else to see. She didn't think she was going to change her whole life.

They made plans. They'd meet tomorrow at seven-thirty, and take the Métro to the cathedral. Afterward, they'd go back to Faith's apartment (Mother would undoubtedly be Out). Then Christmas morning, they'd join Mother and whoever, and have Christmas dinner.

Things did not exactly go according to plan. Faith never met Mother, and she never saw or heard from Bess again after the end of the mass. Faith didn't mind. It was months before she even realized it.

CHAPTER SIX

It was cold Christmas Eve, and the night was so clear Faith could almost believe, the way the ancients had, that the sky was a crystalline sphere. Stars shone around the towers of Notre Dame, peeping at her under the flying buttresses. Everyone, Faith noticed, was walking with his head up, even though this meant stretching necks from the protection of scarves (everybody in France wore scarves all the time) and exposing the flesh to the night air. It was all very beautiful.

Then she reached the cathedral itself. She and Bess found themselves part of a huge, noisy crowd, a sort of sidewalk UN, jostling and shoving, and just generally making itself obnoxious in a dozen languages. Unbidden, the word "rabble" came to mind. She remembered the old movie that had scared her so much when she was a child, with Charles Laughton pouring boiling oil, or molten lead, or *something* unpleasant on the crowd surging below. She was beginning to understand what he had in mind.

Still, the press of bodies tempered the wind. The only part of her that was still freezing was her feet. The sidewalk sucked the heat from them. Faith was aware of them only as a dull ache.

It took forever. Bess got into a mutually incomprehensible conversation with a family of Danes, who seemed to be enjoying the weather. "Do you like Paris?" Bess would ask brightly.

"Ja," the Danes would reply earnestly.

"How long are you going to stay?"

"Ja," the Danes would reply earnestly.

And so forth. Faith tuned out after sixteen Jas, and concentrated on her feet. At one point, there was some excitement

when a shock wave of twisting bodies and bad language(s) made
its way through the crowd. Faith was somewhere near the focus
of the phenomenon, and was nearly knocked off her feet.

"What happened?" Bess demanded. "What happened?"

Amazingly enough, she got an answer from a faceless voice
somewhere in the crowd, speaking English with an accent Faith
couldn't recognize.

"He is wait too long," the voice said. "He is drink too much, so
he make the water. Then he is punch in the mout' by a man,
because he make the water on the trouser of the man."

"Merry Christmas," Faith muttered. Bess said, "Isn't this exciting?"

"These people are supposed to be coming here to *worship.*"

"But it's a *holiday,*" Bess protested.

After that, Faith decided on silence. She knew it was a holiday, and she knew the word holiday came from "holy day," and
this was *Christmas* for God's sake, and these people were supposedly waiting to go to High Mass, and even though she wasn't
much of a Catholic, Faith had more respect for the church, for
the *idea* of church in general, than most of them seemed to.

About nine o'clock, a priest in a black cassock began appearing periodically from an insignificant door behind a fence to
sneak looks at the crowd. Counting the house, maybe, or just
teasing. Faith decided he was trying to be on hand to administer
Last Rites to anyone who might freeze to death.

Faith shifted from foot to foot, and wondered how long it
would take before she became one of his first customers.

At nine-thirty, they opened the huge (maybe fifteen feet
high, six inches thick), metal-studded wooden doors. They
swung back ponderously, but with no noise that could be heard
above the crowd.

Up till now, this expedition had been merely uncomfortable
and inconvenient. Now it became a nightmare.

They rushed the place. As soon as the electrically simulated
candlelight shone through the crack between the doors, this
international gathering of the devout roared like a storm on the
ocean and surged forward like a lynch mob.

Faith knew she and Bess would be separated. Before she'd finished the thought, the mob pinched between them and swept Bess away.

"Wait inside!" Faith screamed. "Inside the door!"

Bess apparently decided it made no sense straining her voice, too. She just nodded emphatically, and gave herself up to the current.

Faith didn't move fast enough, and the press of thousands of heedless bodies pushed her hard into a low stone wall at the base of the fence of metal spears that surrounded the cathedral. The edge of the rock dug cruelly into the back of Faith's calves. She could feel her balance going, but fear of being trampled to death made her fight to keep on her feet.

The only thing to do now was to rush forward herself, become part of the cattle stampede rushing for the big wooden doors, get inside. The idea of being killed trying to get into a church bothered her.

That's when she saw the baby. A dark-haired, dark-eyed little girl, maybe three years old. White tights, patent-leather Mary Janes, and the edge of a pink dress were visible at the bottom of the kid's coat. Her holiday outfit, no doubt. She was probably a pretty child, but it was hard to tell, because now her face was wet with tears and twisted with terror.

The little girl was staggering under the weight of collisions with adult legs. Faith didn't know what was keeping her from falling. Trampling feet drowned out the child's voice, but Faith could read her lips—*maman.*

Apparently, Faith was the only one who could see her, or the only one who cared. Faith began to use her arms and elbows like a Roller Derby queen. She put most of the rest of the crowd to shame. She fought her way to the little girl, and bent to scoop her up in her arms.

Someone beat her to it. The child rose from Faith's field of vision like a lady in a magic trick. A Christmas miracle. Then Faith saw that the child had been swept up into the arms of a tall man in a tan trench coat. In the next few moments, she got to know the trench coat very well, since she planted her nose in the middle of the back of it, and followed it into the church.

There was more room inside the church. Now the shovers became sprinters. The man in the trench coat carried the child (with Faith following) to the lee of a broad stone pillar and stopped. The little girl still called occasionally for *maman,* but the worst of the terror had passed, and she clung to the man for dear life.

"A close call," he said.

Faith nodded. There was still madness around them, but it was the kind of madness she was used to, the madness of Grand Central Terminal at rush hour. Faith took a breath, and looked at the man.

He looked—*nice*. In his thirties, maybe even early thirties. The receding hairline made him look a little older, but there was a twinkle of youth in his eyes. He didn't look handsome, but strong. Secure, kind. The kind of man who would, for instance, risk his life to save a kid from a mob.

He smiled at her, then did a strange thing. He held the baby out to her and said, "Here."

It took Faith a long second before she realized he thought it was her child. "Oh," she said, when the dawn broke. "No. I was just worried—"

"I'm sorry," he said. "I saw you fighting these animals to save the kid, and I figured you must be her mother."

"No. But we have to find her . . ."

That problem was solved immediately. A woman in hysterics ran up to them, and the child leaned toward her, making noises and calling mother. The man handed her the little girl. The woman began to thank God, thank the child's rescuer, express an opinion of Christians who could act that way, and apologize for the inconvenience, all in French, all at once. They told her *Joyeux Noël,* she wished them the same, and, still thanking them over her shoulder, waded back into the crowd to fight them for a seat.

"Well," Faith said. "I guess that's it."

"Yes. I'm glad we didn't have to adopt her."

Faith gave a nervous laugh. "She *is* cute."

"Yes. She is." There was a pause. The cathedral rumbled around them. "Ahh . . . Do you want to look for a couple of seats?"

Yes! Faith thought. "No," she said. "Sorry. I have to find my friend."

"Oh," the man said. Faith was puzzled—he was acting like a high school kid. "How long are you in Paris?"

"I live here."

"Me too. At least for now. Maybe—"

The maybe didn't get finished. Bess came by and dragged her off like a *flic* making an arrest. Faith tried to say something to the man, but the crowds came between them again and blocked them off.

Faith went through the vigil and the mass in a rage. The service itself was beautiful, but many of the people who had risked their lives and those of others to get in left less than halfway through. The game was over, time to go home. And Bess, after having dragged her away from the man in the trench coat, spent the whole service flirting with some Brazilian boy.

After the mass was over, Bess deserted her. It really wasn't right to be away from home on Christmas Eve, she had decided, do come tomorrow, you still have the address, don't you? And off she went into the cold, warmed somewhat, Faith could see, by the arm of the Brazilian boy.

And that's what I get, Faith thought, for taking up with Americans my own age. It was going to be a drag getting home. She knew that with thousands and thousands of people still pouring out of the cathedral, she could never hope to get a taxi (which was what she usually did, late at night), so she set out for the Métro stop, muttering all the way.

Which was closed. She looked at her watch—twenty after one. And the Métro closed at one o'clock. That was on weeknights. On holidays, they probably shut down even earlier.

Faith wasted a few minutes cursing out the French for not making allowances for the holidays, Bess for getting her into this, and herself for not realizing this would happen. She wanted to cry, but that would use energy. She had a nine-mile (fifteen-kilometer) walk through freezing cold and darkness ahead of her. She needed all the energy she could get.

She'd stop at the first cafe she came to, she decided. Get some hot chocolate to fortify herself before they all closed. She gathered her resolve, and faced the necessity of fighting the traffic, pedestrian and vehicular, to get off the Île de la Cité.

A big car pulled up in front of her, and the door sprang open. Faith was startled, and she jumped. A voice from the inside said, "Miss?" It was familiar. She looked inside, and saw the man in the trench coat.

"Can I give you a lift home?" he asked. "I saw you come out of the Métro."

Faith hesitated. God knew she wanted a lift, but Woman Of The World or not, she was still the little girl who'd been told a million times Never To Accept Rides From Strangers.

Of course, he wasn't exactly a stranger. And there was somebody else in the car, a thin, aristocratic-looking old woman. He must, Faith decided, be the chauffeur. He must have risked his job talking his employer into letting him do this. It would be ungrateful to refuse.

She got in the car. "Thanks," she said.

"Don't mention it," he said, beaming at her. Traffic inched forward. "By the way, my name is Paul."

CHAPTER SEVEN

"And so you married him," I said. I worked hard to keep the skepticism out of my voice. I would have plenty of time for skepticism tomorrow—later this morning, actually—when I checked this all out.

"Well, no," Faith said. "Not just like that. There was a lot of stuff that happened first. There was Christmas—in the car, taking me back to Montparnasse, he invited me to the château his family had taken for Christmas. Of course, I found out he wasn't the chauffeur. He didn't have one—he liked to drive, and since he wasn't really spending much time on his business—"

I reminded myself to find out why Paul Letron would spend less time on his business. As long as I was finding things out.

"—he had the time to drive people where they wanted to go. If they didn't want to drive themselves. Or they took cabs. They took a lot of cabs."

Faith shook her head. "I'm getting ahead of myself. I didn't find out anything about the rest of the family until later. That week, I got to know Paul. You wouldn't think you could learn a lot about a person in a week, but you can. We went everywhere —he took me anywhere I asked. I nearly froze him to death on the Eiffel Tower; it was so cold when we went there they wouldn't let us go all the way up, but even from the second level, Paris was so beautiful I didn't want to go back down. When we finally went inside, Paul was practically white. He told me—he told me he was a little anemic."

Faith made eye contact with me, letting me know that what came next was very important. "The thing is, the whole time, he was always a perfect gentleman. He was considerate. He was generous, but he never got lavish and embarrassing. We shook hands when he took me home. What my father used to call a 'Methodist handshake.' He said he got it from Ann Landers. I kept expecting him to make a pass. To tell you the truth, I kept *hoping* he would make a pass. You already know about your sister and me, we were the last of the good girls in high school. A little necking and that was it. We used to talk about it, the two of us. We decided it made sense."

I told her I remembered.

"So you know I'm not cheap or easy or anything. But I liked this man; he was older, and he was attractive, and he was *nice*. He was like the hero of one of those dumb romance novels Mrs. Gold used to hide around the house so no one would know she was reading them, and I was just a dumb kid six months out of high school. I wasn't beautiful, or successful at some career, or anything, but he seemed to be attracted to me. If he wanted to make a pass, I was ready. Where was I?"

Faith rested a hand on her stomach and made a face while she remembered where she was. I wasn't so sure this wasn't a dumb romance, composed on the spot for my benefit, but at the moment, I didn't care. I had to hear how this turned out.

"Oh," Faith said. "On New Year's Eve we gathered at the Eiffel Tower. Not in the tower itself, in the plaza below. It was a lot warmer that night, but it was damp, and I didn't want Paul to risk it if he was anemic, but he insisted.

"I'm glad we went. It was marvelous. When the clock struck twelve, they set off fireworks, and all the people started singing. Some French song. Not 'Auld Lang Syne.' Paul kissed me then for the first time. I was thinking, how silly, of course it wouldn't be 'Auld Lang Syne,' it would be some French song, and all of a sudden, he was kissing me, and I was kissing him, and I thought, how cute, real fireworks. And I was feeling kind of smug, you know, at last he's made his move.

"And that was when he asked me to marry him."

Faith went into a whole lot of romance novel stuff here; Paul Letron, multimillionaire, telling her how lonely he'd been, wrapped up in his work, never stopping to smell the roses, how he knew they'd only known each other a week, but that he'd never felt so sure of anything in his life, etc. It made sense, I told myself. I was trying to be fair. After all, falling in love with a woman was a fairly common emotion, I'd done it a few times myself, and there were only so many ways to get the information across. Bound to be some repetition from time to time.

"But I didn't say yes right away," Faith said.

I said, "Oh." It was as though I'd been caught by an unforeseen plot development.

"He wouldn't let me. It's a good thing, too, because I wouldn't have known what to say. I mean, it sounded like a great idea to me, but I was suspicious of myself for feeling that way so quickly, so I probably would have asked for more time to think things over, anyway."

"But you said yes," I said. "Eventually."

"Of course I did." She patted her stomach. I thought I saw the hint of smile on her face. "But not for another week."

"Another week," I said. That made a great big difference, I thought.

Now it was definitely a smile. She was grinning because she could read my mind. "I know it doesn't sound much different, but I learned a lot in that week."

"Like," I suggested, "you learned who Paul Letron is."

"Exactly!" Faith was talking with real enthusiasm now. The deeper she got into happy memories of Paul Letron, the less she seemed like the terrified fugitive who'd stumbled into my apartment a few hours before. "I mean, I knew he was well off, I saw the car. I saw the house. The clothes, you know what I mean. But I had no idea he had so much *money*. Lucille—Paul's half sister-in-law—left me in a room with a copy of *Forbes* magazine, and I saw that Paul had over *a hundred million dollars!*"

"How did you react to that?" While I waited for a reply, I wondered how I'd react to the news that a hundred million dollars had just asked me to marry it.

"I hated it. I wanted to run away. I wanted to die."

"What kept you around?" I asked.

"Paul did. He came in and saw me holding the magazine, and

he practically fainted. He was going to tell me, he said, but he was afraid to."

Faith told me how Paul had cursed the money, offered to give the money away to charity, anything. It was the *work* he enjoyed; since he wasn't really doing the work anymore, the money didn't really mean that much to him. *(And why isn't he doing the work?* I thought.) How Faith said she didn't believe him, and he'd told her just to say the word, and he'd pick up the phone and do it right away.

"Melodramatic," I said.

"I know how it sounds," Faith said. "It's so *frustrating.* At the time, it all sounded natural. Inevitable, almost."

You had to be there, I thought, but I kept it to myself.

"Anyway," Faith went on, "I couldn't do it. I couldn't tell him to throw all his money away. I mean, he earned it. We left it that we'd work something out."

A good reporter pounces on any hint of a Financial Arrangement. Financial Arrangements have a tendency to go awry. "Did you?" I demanded.

"Did I what?"

"Come to an agreement?"

Faith's expression said, what difference could it possibly make, but she answered the question anyway. "Yes, we did. Just before we got married. A prenuptial agreement. He settled money on me—a trust fund. I get the interest. I get an income from it. A big one. Too much, really. I mean, it's pennies compared to how much there is, but of course it's more than I could ever dream of spending."

"You said you found out a couple of things in the week before you decided to accept Paul's proposal. You mentioned the money. What else?"

"Oh," Faith said. "I'm sorry. It's been so long since I could just *talk* to people, I've forgotten how to do it."

She tightened her lips. "The family. I met his family."

"You wanted to marry him because of his family? From what I've heard so far, I wouldn't rush to have them as in-laws."

"I wanted to marry him because his family was so *awful.* Paul

inherited a small business from his father, and he built it up into
—well, you know what he built it into. And he was stuck with
this terrible woman—I used to call her his wicked stepmother—
and these awful half brothers. Well, some of them are worse
than others, I guess.

"But they acted like he was a buffoon, like he had this freak
talent for making money, which was convenient, because it
enabled these superior creatures to devote themselves to
Higher Things. Am I making any sense?"

"Hank Rearden," I said.

Faith said, "What?"

I told her never mind. "A character in a book who had the
same kind of family." Faith had obviously never read Ayn Rand.

Faith let it go at that. "Not a book I need to read," she said. "I
lived it."

She opened her hands, appealing to reason. "I couldn't leave
Paul alone with that sort of crew. He was—well, he was almost
twice my age, but in some ways, he was a lot younger than I was.
He needed somebody to accept him and care about him and
make him happy. And I did that in the time I had." She said it
with pride. "I really did make him happy."

"The time you had?" I said.

Faith nodded. "About nineteen months. I figured it out once.
Five hundred and seventy-three days."

"Wait a minute." I'm not especially good at math, but you
didn't need a Ph.D. to work this one out. "You said this happened about three years ago."

"Almost exactly three years ago."

"What happened to the other seventeen months? Paul Letron isn't dead—I work for a newspaper, I would have heard
about it. You can't cover up the death of someone as important
as that."

"He's not dead," Faith said. "He's dying. That was the last
thing I found out, you see. Paul was dying of cancer. He's been
in the hospital for seventeen months, a sanitarium, actually,
outside Paris. About a year ago, he slipped into a coma. He's
been on the edge of death for months. He could go any second."

"Wait a minute." I was up out of my chair, looming over her. This was, at last, too much. "Wait just a damn minute. What are you trying to pull?"

Faith looked hurt.

"I can add. If your husband's been in a coma for a year, what are you doing *eight months pregnant?*"

I had to admit the question had a less devastating effect on her than I would have expected.

"That's the point, Harry," she said.

I swallowed hard and forced myself to be calm. *"What* is the point, Faith?"

"The baby. The pregnancy. Paul and I wanted children. I wanted to have one right away, but Paul still had hopes of a miracle cure or something. He wanted to wait so he could be a whole father. That's what he used to say. He watched his own father dying, and he didn't want to put a child of his through that."

"But that doesn't—"

"I arranged for artificial insemination."

"You what?"

"I didn't want to lose Paul before I'd given him a baby, and he didn't want his child to remember his father, if at all, as an invalid. So Paul had some of his sperm frozen and told me that if he ever got so sick it looked as if he were never coming out of the hospital, that I should use it. If I wanted to.

"If I wanted to, for God's sake! As if I ever wanted anything else.

"But that's why they're after me, you see."

"The family," I said.

"Exactly. I waited too long, but for months, I hoped against hope Paul would come out of the coma."

I took a breath. "And they didn't know—"

"No," Faith said, and her voice was acid. "They'd had three months, after Paul lapsed into a coma, to get used to the idea of being his heirs. They're his only relatives, after all. I don't count —the money Paul arranged for me is beyond their reach, and it's negligible to them, anyway."

"But with a child . . ." I felt very wise. Look out for those Financial Arrangements.

"My child will inherit what his father intended him—or her— to have. It's most of the estate. Not all of it. His will provides for his family handsomely. More money than any sane person could want.

"But they're not sane people. They hate me for showing Paul how much better he was—is—than they are. They want all his money, all of it they can get their hands on.

"They tried to give me poison just before I left Paris. They followed me to New York. They're spending Paul's money on a huge suite at the Westbrook. Since they've arrived, I've been nearly pushed off a subway platform. Tonight, I was nearly run over by a car.

"Because if I die, my baby will die. And they're convinced they can't afford to let my baby live!"

CHAPTER EIGHT

If anyone had asked me, I would have said I didn't get any sleep, but in the morning, Faith told me she heard me snoring on the frequent occasions she left the other bedroom to go to the bathroom. All I know is, awake or asleep, I was thinking about Faith Sidon and her little problem.

It even did me some good. I woke up with plans, and I got right to work on them. The first thing I did was to call The Grayness and tell them I'd be in late today. Nobody minded. One of the (few) good things about my job is that as long as the work gets done, nobody cares when I do it, even if I drop in in the middle of my vacation. The next step was a call to Scarsdale, to tell my mother I had a surprise for Sue, and that she should call me the second she got home. Faith, meanwhile, was polishing off a bowl of instant farina. Straight, almost. Just a little sugar and milk.

"I thought you were just having a baby," I told her. "I didn't know you had to eat like one."

"If you don't like farina, why do you keep it around the house?"

"I like it fine," I told her. "I consider it a vehicle for butter, and maple syrup, or brown sugar, or fruit, or nuts, or jam, or a combination of any of that."

She smiled. "Why didn't you tell your mother?"

"Tell her what?"

"That I'm here. That it was really me on the phone last night?"

"Strategy," I said.

Faith left it at that, but there was a look on her face that said she'd like to know what I meant. It was a good, wholesome look of honest curiosity, and it looked especially nice on a face that had had a night's rest and a good morning scrub. It was a face to feel brotherly toward. If I could only forget her story from last night, I could have enjoyed it.

At eleven o'clock, my sister called.

Sue and I have this game we play. We call it "Wasp," but a better name would be "1950s Sitcom Family." The winner is the last one to crack up.

"Hiya, Sis!" I gushed, as soon as I heard her voice on the phone.

"Hiya, Har!" she said. "Gee, it sure is swell to hear your voice!" Every declarative sentence in a Wasp game ends with an exclamation point.

"Yeah, I know how it can be, burning the old midnight oil, trying to get that sheepskin!"

"You said it, brother dear! What can I do you for?"

"Wake up and smell the kaaffee!" I thought I heard a giggle on the other end. That phrase, and that pronunciation, usually did the job, but Sue was apparently getting tougher. "It's what I can do *you* for!"

"Wow!" she said. "I bet you're about the best brother in the *whole world!*"

The next sound was laughter. Mine. Sue said, "Hah! Gotcha. Good thing, too. I couldn't have taken much more of that, myself."

"I don't blame you."

"Well, I am touched, and everything, but what's up? I mean, why was I supposed to call you the second I came through the door? Do I have to tell you Mom is having kittens?"

"When is she not? *Did* you call the second you came through the door?"

"I took my coat off first."

"Oh," I said. "Too bad."

"For God's sake, Harry, what—"

"I've got a surprise for you," I said, and I handed the phone to Faith.

This was where the strategy came in. I spring Faith on my

sister, and of course she gets all gooey about it, and has to rush into the city, right away, which is what I wanted. The advantage is, *I* don't have to be the one to talk my mother into letting it happen, which can be a production—you just got here, now you're rushing off, what's your hurry, sure, go, I'm just your mother—need I go on? Sue has always been better at dealing with Mom than I have, anyway.

It was arranged. Sue would drive to White Plains and take the next train in. I tried to get Faith to tell Sue we'd meet her at Grand Central, but I couldn't get her attention. Or she was ignoring me. It didn't really matter that much. Sue knew where I lived; she even had a key. She'd take a cab, it would take fifteen extra minutes.

Meanwhile, they talked. Faith neglected to mention she was pregnant, which, I decided, would make for an amusing reunion scene. Faith finally said, "The sooner we hang up, the sooner you can get here," and put the phone back. She was smiling when she turned to me.

"We could have met her at Grand Central," I said.

The smile slid from Faith's face like an egg from a Teflon pan. "No. It's too dangerous."

I could feel my own smile wither and die. "Right," I said.

"Not just for me," Faith said. "I couldn't stand to have anything happen to you or Sue."

I told her that was very considerate of her.

"You don't believe me," she said. Her voice was amazed.

"It's a pretty remarkable story," I told her.

"But, Harry," she said, "it's *me!*"

"If it wasn't you, I would have called the men in the white coats long ago."

"Don't bother," she said. "I'll just leave. I—I'll call and tell Sue where to meet me." The idea now was for her to leap to her feet and stride regally from the room, but practically all of that was out of the question for a woman as pregnant as Faith. Especially one with a bum hand, useless even for levering her out of the chair.

"Grow up. Stay put. Listen. Faith, if I disappeared for three years, then came back breathless, saying Prince Rainier had put the Monégasque Secret Service on me because I'd been shacking up with Princess Stephanie, wouldn't you want to see a little evidence first?"

"Don't be ridiculous!"

"You wouldn't? Well, you are well named. You have a lot more faith than most people."

"I mean your story is ridiculous."

I didn't say anything. She listened to herself, then took a step outside her own emotions and ran her story through again. Finally she said, "But it's *true!*"

"I'm not saying it's not."

"But you want evidence. I don't have any evidence!"

"I'll find the evidence. You just relax. If you're telling the truth—"

"I am!"

"—the best thing for you to do is relax. Just let me check things out."

"How long is that going to take?"

"A day. I work for a newspaper, remember?"

She didn't say anything, but she didn't leave, either. The atmosphere remained perceptibly cool until my sister arrived.

CHAPTER NINE

Those who can, do. Those who can't, teach. Those who can't teach, teach teachers.

And those who can't teach teachers become specialty journalists.

Herbert (Don't Call Me "Herb") Helverson was, if you can believe it, a more pathetic Grayness case history than I was. He was a couple of years older than I was, and had a bit more seniority, so every now and then, the Powers That Be not only let him write something, they even put it in the paper. Once, they even gave him a byline.

The big difference between us was, Herbert *loved* what he was doing. He did various tables, charts and graphs for the Sunday Business Section, and he called companies to check spellings of names of guys who had recently been promoted to vice president, so the captions on the little mug shots they ran would be correct.

This would be like giving an eleven-year-old kid the job of calling ballplayers to check the spelling of their names for the bubble-gum cards, and letting him make the lists on the backs. Herbert was just stone in love with Business, got a thrill from it. Kept track of it, followed it, just the way I followed the NFL.

The similarity went deeper than that. There was a certain amount of wistfulness going on, too. Just as I would give two years off my life to have enough ability to play for the Giants, Herbert would kill or die to be able to once in his life make an investment that didn't go sour. He was the kind of guy, who, if he'd been around in the late forties, would have put his life savings into frozen radio dinners. To put it in sports terms, he had the desire, but not the touch. Actually, once or twice I had to help him balance his checkbook.

I went to the Sunday Business Section office as soon as I got to The Grayness after I left Faith in the custody of my sister.

That reunion had been something to see. Sue had walked in, smiled at me, then got a look at Faith. I never believed people's eyes could actually bug out before. Sue, with the typical Ross perspicacity, had said, "You're pregnant," just in case Faith hadn't previously been aware of it, then ran to her and gave her a big hug.

Then they started to babble. They always had. It used to amaze me—I don't think either of them has ever completed a sentence in the presence of the other.

"Why didn't you—"

"Because I didn't want—"

"But your best friend, I mean—"

"I missed you, but—"

Like that. I knew they were good for hours, so I just told them not to leave the apartment until I got back. Sue wanted to know why. With her brother, she completes sentences.

"Faith will tell you all about it," I promised, and left, locking the door behind me. I smiled as I went down in the elevator. This would be something else that would keep them in the apartment—Faith would tell Sue what a beast I was, and Sue, being a younger sister, would have to agree. That meant she'd have to take Faith's story for gospel, and that would keep them in the apartment until I knew *what* the hell I wanted to believe. Herbert Helverson was supposed to help me out with that.

Herbert was hunched over his computer terminal, cackling away about the strength of the dollar, especially with the drop in the prime rate. "You just watch," he said, before he could have known I was there. "You just watch. Parity with the Pound. It's coming. A year, two years, it's coming." He patted the gray-painted machine like the flank of a faithful horse. He really loved that computer.

I know it makes sense for the Business Section (daily or Sunday, though they pretend to be deadly enemies with nothing in common) to have computers to work with, but these things have taken over The Grayness. We're supposed to be the World's Greatest Newspaper, but the only actual paper in the place anymore is in the bathrooms.

I coughed. Herbert turned, pushing his half-glasses up his nose as he did. There was always something vaguely Victorian about him, with his narrow face, and lank hair, and high collars and pinstriped suits.

"Harry," he said. He sounded glad to see me. He always sounded glad to see me. All of the business reporters had money in something or other (remember that the next time you read an impartial report on coming trends), and they tended to avoid Herbert's company, considering him somewhat of a jinx. "What brings you around here? I already had lunch."

"Me too," I lied. "No, I'd just like a favor. Some background on a business and some of the management."

"You sound like you're looking for investment advice." The idea of someone asking him for investment advice hit him, and he gave three loud, short barks of laughter. Then he was grave, awed by the potential responsibility. "You're not, are you?"

"Does the dollar really look that good?" I asked him.

"Absolutely. I'm going to take a bath on those pounds I bought in April. Who wants to buy them now?"

"Why don't you just hang on to them, and go to Britain on your vacation."

"That won't make up for the money I lost."

"No, but you'll still get a pound's worth of merchandise for them."

He looked at me as if I were suddenly speaking Tagalog. To a lot of these Business Section guys, economics is like tic-tac-toe, a game played on paper with no application to the real world. I decided to let it go, or there was no telling when I'd get out of there.

"Tell me about Paul Letron and Letronique Cosmetics."

Herbert squinted at me, first through his lenses, then over the top of them. "Why do you want to know about him?"

"Personal curiosity. I met someone who says he knows him."

"During the last three years?"

"Mmm hmm."

"Who is this person? Can I talk to him?"

"I don't know," I said. Not now, he couldn't, at any rate. "Why?"

"The man is the talk of the business world. I mean, he was before he disappeared, but since, it's been intense."

"What do you mean?"

"Well, look at him. He's only *four years older* than you are—you're twenty-nine, right?"

"Right," I said.

"And he's the same age I am," Herbert said in tones of reverence, "and he's already been in the *Forbes* 400. Twice."

"Shall I genuflect? Or can I just bow my head?"

Herbert had no sense of humor, so he rarely knew when he was being put on. I mean, I have enormous respect for people who make honest money in business—I read Ayn Rand (speaking of no sense of humor), and mostly, I even buy her. But this wasn't respect, this was worship. I know I should have been expecting it from the man who had his copy of *Iacocca* bound in leather, but it was still a bit much.

"You don't have to do anything, Harry." Herbert took it absolutely deadpan. "Not being in business, you don't know what the man has done to inspire such respect in me."

"That's one of the reasons I came here," I told him. "To find out."

Herbert nodded. Sounded fair enough to him. "There are some terrific businessmen out there, geniuses, some of them, artists. Paul Letron is one of them. He went into a cutthroat business. Cosmetics is murder. It has to be, because the stuff these people make is all the same; the only difference is the image; the image is everything—and he carved out an enormous share of it by the time he was twenty-eight. By the time he was thirty-three, he was one of America's richest men, in charge of a multinational he built himself. And he still owns most of it. Astounding."

"You said he was even more astounding since he dropped out of sight."

"He is."

"Care to elaborate?"

"Well, the company's doing as well as ever, better. They get memos, they do what they say, and they make money. But nobody ever sees Letron anymore, or even talks to him on the phone."

"Like Howard Hughes."

"Not exactly. That's the weird stuff."

"Weirder than Howard Hughes? Come on, Herbert."

"It's not that. It's just that we keep hearing rumors about him."

"Come on," I said again. "I'm about as far removed from journalism as you can get and still work for a newspaper, and even *I* hear rumors."

"Yes, but these rumors . . ."

"Yeah?"

"They keep checking out."

A little moving sign went across my vision in lights: HOLY SHIT!!! SHE TOLD THE TRUTH!!!

I made my voice calm. "What kind of rumors, Harry?"

"Oh, like he was living in this big villa in Italy, helping peasants on the estate crush grapes . . ."

"And he was?" I was feeling vindicated. If this was a rumor that checked out, I could haul Faith off to a shrink with a clear conscience.

"He had been. He cleared out before a reporter could get there. But the peasants all confirmed the story, grapes and all." He looked at me as if he were disappointed in me. "We ran the story, Harry, in *Business People*. I wrote it up. Don't you read your own paper?"

I did not actually tell him to shut up. I was thinking, cleared out of Italy, went where? France did present itself.

"Tell me another rumor that checked out, Herbert," I said.

"Well, he got married. To a teenager. Young American girl. From Westchester, I think."

"You're kidding, right?"

"I could think of a million better things to kid about."

I wanted to get this straight. "Now, Herbert. We are talking about *the* Paul Letron? Let Us Make Your Face Fabulous? Your hero?"

"Of course. Are you all right, Harry?"

"I'm terrific. You wouldn't happen to have this teenager's name, would you?"

"Just a second." He punched a few buttons. "Here it is: Faith Sidon, U.S.A. First marriage for each. Our reporter got an affidavit from the man who performed the ceremony, and he got the number of the marriage certificate. The reporter saw it with his own eyes. We ran this story, too." He was beginning to sound genuinely hurt.

"I can't believe it."

"We did, Harry. I'll send down to the morgue for the microfilm."

"No. I can't believe about the wedding."

"Why not? Rich older men have been marrying teenagers for centuries. I suspect getting to sleep with teenagers is one of the best parts about getting rich." He sighed, probably realizing he'd never know unless he hit the lottery, and Business Section reporters make it a point of honor never to play the lottery. Too risky.

Herbert looked off into the distance like a mystic. "I wonder what he's up to now."

"Yeah," I said, "me too," but I had a pretty good feeling I already knew. Paul Letron was holding down a hospital bed in some French nursing home, in an irreversible coma, waiting to die, or waiting for his child to be born, if enough brain cells remained active for him to remember the plan.

The moving sign cut across my vision again, only this time there were more exclamation points behind the holy shit.

I was of the True Faith, now. Oh, there were still things to check out, and I was going to check them, but it would be a formality. I was a believer. I had latched on (just like a real reporter!) to a great big story.

The question now was, what was I going to do with it?

CHAPTER TEN

It was about three o'clock in the afternoon when I walked up to the desk in the Westbrook Hotel and asked if any of the Letrons was at home.

The Westbrook was a carven pile of granite near Central Park that had been catering to the needs of the Best People (and also to the merely rich) for nearly a hundred years. It was a small piece of the feudal system surrounded by New York's howling democracy.

The desk clerk was a young Korean version of the Great Gildersleeve. He did not say "Nyaaaass?" but he did demand everything short of a birth certificate and a loyalty oath before parting with any information. What he told me was that none of the Letrons was in. He wouldn't tell me what room they were out of.

"The Guests, after all," he said, with one of the best Hollywood-British accents I've ever heard, "pay a premium for service and privacy." He pronounced it "privvacy."

It was all very commendable, and I told him so. There was a whole lot of other stuff I would have liked to tell him, but I held it in. I was crippled by the code of The Grayness. Remember all those great old newspaper movies they used to make? Where reporters would go undercover to expose wrongdoing, grease the wheels of the great machine of public information with a few judiciously applied bucks, and in the end, wind up duking it out with the bad guys and handing them over to the cops?

Well, forget it. The code of The Grayness fixes it so that the only fun a reporter can have is when one of the people he exposes (usually by printing stolen documents provided by the victim's jealous colleague) resigns or commits suicide. The code of The Grayness forbids: (a) paying anybody money for information under any circumstances; (b) using a false name; (c) using a false occupation; (d) using in a story any material you got from anybody who did not know you were a reporter for The Grayness. This is supposed to protect the Sacred Honor of The Grayness, but what it does, of course, is turn the reporters into fences for stolen documents. It also provides more evidence for the theory that movies are infinitely superior to real life.

Even I (as I was given to understand the day The Grayness bestowed upon me the honor of allowing me to do its TV listings) was bound by the code. A violation, like if I pretended to be Ronald Reagan and called a station to ask if one of my old movies was on tonight, would be cause for instant dismissal. Yes, I know I hated the job. That didn't mean I wanted to be fired. Looks bad on the resume.

I did the only thing I could do. I told a lie not covered by the code. "Are you sure they're not in?" I said. I raised an eyebrow when I said it. It takes a snob to deal with a snob.

"Quite sure," he said.

"Then why are there no keys in their box? Surely people as important as this would want their messages taken while they are out."

The desk clerk looked at me as if he suspected I was some sort of venomous insect. Then he looked in the box. The box positively rattled with keys, and I was suitably embarrassed. I gave him my Harvard apology—the one that implied that it was your fault, you swine, you were out to make me look like a fool, and it's only my impeccable breeding that keeps me from thrashing you within an inch of your worthless and undoubtedly illegitimate life.

The good news was that I now knew what room they were in. The Imperial Suite, twelfth floor.

Then I had to decide what I should do next. I had lots of exciting ideas, most of them so underhanded that The Grayness had never even thought to forbid them. I could sneak up the service stairs. Pick the lock of the suite. Check the garbage cans for stuff. Torn-up pictures of babies. Bloodstained rent-a-car contracts. Like that.

Sanity, however, prevailed over my sense of fun. I had to put things in perspective. Faith could be married to Paul Letron and still be crazy. Or even misled by a series of nasty coincidences. I wanted to talk to these people, size them up. The last thing I wanted to do was get them paranoid by running around letting all the hotel employees know I was interested. No. I take it back. The last thing I wanted was to be caught tossing the suite of the family of a millionaire financier. Let's be honest here—I was new at this, and more than a little nervous about what I might be getting into.

I decided to wait for them, at least for a little while. If they were shopping (which was a good bet in this neighborhood), they could well be back soon. Also, the Korean Gildersleeve would undoubtedly tell them some maniac had been asking about them; it would be a good idea to get in there with my explanation as soon as possible.

It would help, of course, if I knew what they looked like. I called my apartment. Sue answered. I asked how they were doing.

Sue said, "Great, we're making bread pudding."

"How's Faith getting along?"

"Fine. Pretty amazing stuff, isn't it?" Faith would hear that and think Sue was talking about bread pudding.

"Amazing, but at least partially true."

"Really?"

"Really. Let me talk to Faith."

Sue put her on. I told her I'd been to the paper.

"And?"

"And it checks out. I do not apologize for doubting you, but I'm not surprised you think I should. Can we leave it that I'm glad the doubts were wrong, and be friends again?"

"We were always friends."

"Good. Describe your in-laws for me."

She wanted to know why, but I said I'd tell her later. We must have been friends. She bought it right away, and gave me five thumbnail sketches. I thanked her, told her to save me some of the pudding, and hung up. Then I tightened The Grayness's financial hold on me by making two credit-card phone calls to Europe. After that, I went to the Westbrook's famous Willow Room, where I sat at a marble-topped table facing the door and waited for the Letrons to show up.

I drank tea and ate crumpets with lemon curd while I waited, paying a fortune for them. Something I discovered during my junior year abroad is that the stuff Americans imagine the British Aristocracy eating while they run around the house in tuxedos, is actually consumed for breakfast at the kitchen table by guys in torn sweaters who need a shave. They eat it because it's cheap.

Nothing could be cheap at the Westbrook, of course, or even economical, but at least it was good.

Good timing, too. I was just finishing up the second cup of tea (the Westbrook serves you in a two-cup pot) when a few bells went off, and three bellhops hastened to the brass-and-glass front door to aid the doorman with some packages. When the door swung open, I could see a driver in the discreetest possible gray pop out of a Rolls-Royce much the same color, and dash around opening doors.

The car disgorged a strikingly handsome woman with silver-streaked black hair and three blonds, two men and a woman with the tall, cool good looks of a Candice Bergen. Not *all* the tall, cool good looks of a Candice Bergen—she was no movie star, or anything. She would, however, do, until one came along.

This had to be Lucille, the wife of Paul's half brother Robert. Robert himself was not among us, it seemed, unless he had shaved off the golden beard Faith had told me about. That seemed unlikely, though. Like many fair-haired men, Robert had had to wait the best part of nine months before the growth on his face looked like a beard rather than a skin disease, and he had taken ceaseless teasing from his wife and siblings (Paul always excepted, according to Faith) while he was waiting.

So, assuming someone who put up with that kind of crap to grow a beard would keep it around awhile before he got rid of it, I assumed the two blond young men were Louis (twenty-seven) and Peter (twenty-two), Alma's sons by Paul's father.

I must admit they were impressive. The young people (Lucille, I had been surprised to find out, was younger than I was, and the missing Robert was only thirty), tall and clean and golden the way they were, looked like nothing so much as a bunch of Thals, those incredibly virtuous and beautiful characters from "Doctor Who," who managed to evolve on the same planet as the disgustingly evil Daleks.

Alma looked like Circe, although from the way she skewered a bellhop with her eye when he jostled a package, she wasn't the type to be content merely to turn men into swine. She'd turn them into *porc à la Boulangère*, and then eat them.

Grandly, they turned their backs on the hired help struggling under the weight of their purchases, and walked grandly into the elevator. The interesting thing about the whole process was the fact that none of them made the slightest noise—they seemed to glide across the carpet (a Dalek trait, actually), and they never uttered a sound. All the way across the vast Westbrook lobby, their lips never parted. It was as if they were walking around with mouthfuls of liquid gold, and they didn't want to spill a drop.

I would have to find some way to make them change their minds about that.

CHAPTER ELEVEN

I spent the trip up in the elevator concocting elaborate plans to get the Letrons to let me inside their suite. I wasn't, after all, a cop or anything. And it could be safely inferred from what Herbert Helverson had told me that Faith's in-laws (her real, honest-to-God in-laws, I had to keep telling myself) were a little shy around reporters. But I had to talk to them. Somebody had to, and there were two reasons I didn't think trying to persuade a cop to do it would be a good idea. One, Faith had already tried it, with no success, and two, while I might be able to get a more respectful response from the police with the awe and might of The Grayness behind me and the evidence that at least part of Faith's story was true, I just plain didn't want to.

I think I was concentrating on ways to get the door open in an unsuccessful attempt to keep from speculating about the *reasons* I didn't want to. Could it be I didn't like the idea of my sister's best friend married to a hundred-millionaire? Did Faith's admission that she'd once had a crush on me awaken some unholy and previously unadmitted passion a teenaged Harry Ross had conceived for the sub-teen Faith Sidon all those years ago? Or was it something else, like a recurrence of journalistic ambition, stifled (I thought) since I had gotten such an intimate knowledge of how the working press worked?

This was, let's not kid anybody, one hot story. Herbert Helverson had shown me that. I had left him wiping drool spots from his terminal just at the idea that I had met and spoken to someone who'd even *seen* Paul Letron since the big disappearance. Could I be looking at this situation, not as a way to help an old friend, but as my ticket off the TV listings and on to better things?

I decided it was just that after a lifetime of mystery stories and science fiction and swashbucklers, I was in this for the adventure. Besides, there was nothing to say the cops wouldn't laugh at me, too. In the current state of my life, I didn't need cops (or anybody) laughing at me.

Despite all this, or maybe because of it, by the time I walked up to the door, I still had no idea how I was going to get inside.

It turned out to be just as well I didn't show up at the door carrying a pizza, or ring the bell (the rooms had doorbells at the Westbrook) and announce Avon Calling. For want of a better idea, I simply pressed the button. I heard chimes from inside the suite, then the sound of a peephole cover being slid back (rooms at the Westbrook also had peepholes in the doors). A soft, low, throaty voice said, "Yes?" The owner of the voice had undoubtedly intended it to sound sexy, and hadn't entirely failed. The only thing undecided was what sex.

I said, "Good afternoon. My name is Ross. I'd like to come in and talk with you for a few moments." I put a rising inflection on the end of the sentence, enough to remove the curse of making a demand, but not enough to make an actual request out of it. The idea was to convince everyone concerned, including myself, that I actually had a right to be here.

"I'm afraid—" the voice began. I was trying to decide which of the men or women I'd seen downstairs was the owner of the voice. Whoever it was, it sounded amused, maybe a little tipsy.

I didn't give it a chance to tell me what it was afraid of. Still polite, I added, "It's about Faith."

"I wasn't aware they let Jehovah's Witnesses solicit in the Westbrook."

I raised an eyebrow. It took me hours in front of a mirror when I was a kid to learn how to do that, so I hoped the owner of the voice could see it through the peephole. I can also pat my head and rub my stomach at the same time.

"Faith Letron," I said. "The former Faith Sidon. The wife," I added, "of Paul Letron."

"Oh," the voice said. "The Waif. Just a second."

The peephole clapped shut, and I could hear the oiled click of locks and the dull rattle of a chain bolt.

It occurred to me after my previous mental gymnastics that the whole process was easier than it should have been. I mean, they didn't even ask me what about her. I had accomplished a lot for just one raised eyebrow. I was still okay as far as the Code of The Grayness went, because I hadn't asked anything that would produce an answer that might be published.

The hardware noises stopped, followed by a silence that took considerably longer than a second. It took longer than the entire conversation through the door had.

I had just about concluded that they beat it down the fire escape. I decided this was a good thing, since flight is evidence of guilt. At least I thought it was. Perry Mason always said it was. My mother always says I should have gone to law school (like every time I complain about The Grayness), and for the first time, I was beginning to see some merit in her arguments.

Before I could get this one completely worked out, the door swung open, and I walked in on what looked like a hastily called convention. The room was rich and dark, like something on the ground floor of a Victorian mansion instead of something near the top of a pile of Manhattan concrete. It was paneled in oak, and the furniture (which consisted of either genuine antiques or damned good reproductions) was upholstered in a subdued blue. The fabric wasn't actually worn, just old enough to avoid looking as if someone actually intended it to be used in a hotel.

The ceiling as probably fourteen feet high, with decorations. It wasn't the Sistine Chapel or anything, just carvings of grapes and the occasional faun. The kind of job that fed an immigrant woodcarver's family for a month or two back around the turn of the century.

Faith had told me that her husband's family never stayed at the Westbrook for more than a few days, while the staff at the main house in Connecticut got the place ready for occupancy. Faith had never stayed at the Connecticut place herself, but she'd gotten the impression from the way Paul talked about it that it made the château outside Paris look like a shack.

I wondered how much per day it cost to rent this suite. And I wondered at the kind of mentality that could spend that kind of money (it had to be astronomical, whatever it was) just to keep a roof overhead for a few days while you waited to get back to your mansion.

I tried to imagine the kind of people who'd seem natural in a place like this. Arab oil sheikhs. Royalty. People with names like Cadwallader St. Buffington III. It occurred to me that the one thing they had in common was the fact that none of them earned money for themselves. That must make a difference. Even if I become rich, so rich I can buy The Grayness itself, I don't think I really see myself deliberately staying in a suite like this. That's not to say I won't develop a letch for carved oak walls and ceilings, or something equally extravagant. One of the nice things about having a lot of money, I deduce on the basis of the amount I already do make, is being able to work up an enthusiasm for buying things you don't really need. But I doubt I'll ever get so attached that I'll have to *rent* the stuff during the few days I'm between houses and out of touch with my own.

Of course, as far as I'm concerned, if I can't be home with my books and my tapes, I'd just as soon be in a Holiday Inn, where I know there's a good TV in the room and the showers are hot. I had no right to judge the Letrons by my own disgustingly bourgeois standards. Anyway, by the criterion I'd just established, these people *did* belong here. It was Paul Letron and his father who'd done all the earning. Faith didn't like them, but all my actions today were based on the possibility that Faith could be some kind of paranoid nut. I certainly didn't want to let Faith's attitude prejudice me. For all I knew, the Letrons were perfectly nice people.

From the looks on their faces, though, the odds were against it.

"What has The Waif to say?" It was the owner of the voice. Lucille, this was, the younger of the two women I'd see downstairs; tall, blond, high cheekbones. The look explained the voice, or at least went with it. Lucille had been exposed to a lot of old movies, apparently, and had decided at an early age to be

Lizabeth Scott, or if she got lucky, Tallulah Bankhead. I wasn't surprised to see the full makeup at three o'clock in the afternoon, or the high heels, or the shiny gray silk dress. I wondered where the foot-long cigarette holder was.

She was certainly looking me over the way a movie siren would. Slowly, with no shame. She kept looking at my hair. Aside from a little premature gray at the temples, there is nothing special about my hair. It began to get on my nerves.

Everything about her began to get on my nerves. The crooked little amused smile she gave me, the dirty chuckle in her voice when she asked me to come in. Everything about her seemed to say "Let's see what *you* can offer in the way of amusement." She was the kind of woman to whom a man develops an irresistible urge to teach a thing or two. I keep running into them. I don't think I've managed to teach them much.

"The Waif?" I said.

"That's what we call her." Lucille Letron told me her name, then sat on a gilt chair composed primarily of circles and curlicues. It suited her, but it seemed too fragile to support even her slender weight. "It's more or less a joke. Isn't it, Louis?"

He'd just entered the room. Louis Letron, according to Faith, could be charming, practically irresistible. He worked (when he could be persuaded to work) for the family business, training sales personnel. Paul had always said he did a very good job, but that he could do one of the best, if he would only devote as much energy to the business as he did pursuing his hobby. Paul had never told Faith what Louis's hobby was, but it didn't take her long to figure it out for herself. It was dark-skinned women —Oriental, Hispanic, African, Arabic, good sun tan, it didn't seem to matter. As long as she was beautiful, intelligent, and dark, there was no limit to the amount of time, money, and effort he would spend to get her into bed with him, presumably because he liked the contrast. Then, he'd lose interest, until another caught his eye.

"Isn't what?" Louis asked.

"A joke. Calling her The Waif."

He smiled with everything from the neck up. Even his hair

seemed to get shinier. "Well, it was sort of funny, Paul's bringing her home after someone had abandoned her on the church steps, as it were, and her walking around mooning after him like a kid from a Charlie Chaplin movie or something . . ."

He paused as if he'd just thought of something. "Oh. I'm Louis Letron, by the way." He stuck out his hand.

"Harry Ross," I said, taking it.

"Mr. Ross wants to talk to us about Faith, Louis."

"Why us? I mean, she was a lovely child, but for all we lived in the same house—I mean all of us, now, the whole family—we never really got to know her."

Louis was really pumping out the charm, now. No hard feelings, some people hit it off, some don't. Nothing to get excited over.

Like many people who wouldn't know how to be charming if our lives depended on it, I am frequently suspicious of people who do.

"Isn't her baby what stands between you people and the bulk of your half brother's money? And control of Letronique Cosmetics?"

There was a little gasp from Lucille, but her brother-in-law's charm stood up just fine. "Why, that's ridiculous!" he said. He was just short of laughter.

"I think you should leave, Mr. Ross," Lucille said. Louis let the mask drop for a split-second, just long enough to shoot his sister-in-law a look that said why did you let him in in the first place?

"Our future—and I can speak with confidence for the family on this topic, Mr. Ross—is secure. Both in and out of Letronique Cosmetics. It is true, the child Faith is carrying stands to receive the bulk of my brother's estate. As you probably know, he has been unwell."

That was a nice way to express a months-long coma and an inoperable tumor, I thought. Unwell. This, undoubtedly, was a direct descendent of the people who used to describe the Civil War as "the late unpleasantness."

"But bulk or no bulk, he has not forgotten us. We are well provided for, all of us. And as far as the company goes, we will retain enough voting stock to keep our jobs—my brother Robert and I work for the company, as you undoubtedly know—and the traditional family seat on the board of directors as long as we desire."

"Faith was always hard to figure out," Lucille said. It was hard to think a woman like her could efface herself so successfully, but she had. I almost jumped when she spoke. "She seemed to think she'd walked into some Gothic novel or something; always acting like an outsider, misinterpreting all our efforts to make her feel at home. When Paul couldn't run the business anymore, and had to be hospitalized, she wouldn't reach out to us. She wouldn't let us reach out to her, either.

"Of course we were upset when she had that horrible medical experiment done to her—"

"You mean artificial insemination?"

That was what she'd meant, all right. She shuddered when I said the words. I thought she was a little out of date, but everyone to his own hang-up.

I was thinking there was nothing to this investigative reporter business. One rude sentence, and these people opened up like Joe E. Brown's mouth. I decided to try another.

"So you've always been nice to her."

Louis looked sheepish. Charmingly sheepish. "Well, I did tease her, at first. Until I found out how sensitive she was. To my eternal shame, I was the first person to call her The Waif."

"But you've never done anything to justify her belief that one or all of you is trying to kill her."

I expected a bigger laugh out of Lucille, but what I got was a snort. Louis, apparently, was speechless.

"She thinks we're trying to kill her?" Lucille's voice cracked —it wasn't designed for the higher notes of skepticism.

"Or cause a miscarriage," I said.

"That's why you came here?"

"I wanted to ask you about it."

"Are you a policeman?" Louis was deferential.

I told him I wasn't.

"You must be Faith's psychiatrist," Lucille said. "Well, to answer your question, yes, she is crazy. Kill her, for God's sake!"

"I'm not a psychiatrist," I said. "I'm a reporter from The Grayness."

You might have thought I'd said I was a kiddie porn vendor. I'd never spoken a sentence with greater impact, and I never thought I'd get such a kick out of following the code of The Grayness.

"After all," I said, "The Grayness wouldn't want to print anything that wasn't true."

CHAPTER TWELVE

"That is nonsense, young man." It was an icicle of a voice—cold, clear, and sharp. It chilled the room.

It was Alma Letron, the wicked stepmother. Circe, I'd thought downstairs. She had changed from street clothes, and was now dressed for the part. She was wearing a sort of purple-red lounging robe that went from her collarbone to the floor. It hid her feet, making the Dalek comparison even stronger. Faith had told me that Alma was fifty years old or close to it, but that glide was still something to see.

Louis and Lucille did everything but curtsy and bow as Alma made her way across the hotel's carpet and sat down. She chose another antique wooden chair to sit in. This one had a high back, and upholstered arms. It didn't especially look like a throne until she sat in it.

"Nonsense," she said again. "How many times must I repeat myself, Mr. Ross? I know you're not mute; your foolishness has been resounding all through the suite."

It was a little early in our acquaintance for me to call such a queenly individual a liar, but that's what she was. I can shout, but I hadn't been shouting then, and I doubted the Westbrook would be pleased to hear such a valued customer promulgating a canard about their world-famous soundproofing.

"You must be Alma Letron," I said, just to let her know I wasn't intimidated. Or not to let her know I *was* intimidated. It bothered me I couldn't decide which.

She didn't bother to acknowledge. "I already know who you are. You say your newspaper never prints anything that isn't true."

"I said we don't *want* to print anything that isn't true. Sometimes it happens anyway."

She sniffed. "Yes, like that disgraceful business about Baro."

"Who?"

"Baro. He's a sculptor. A genius. He was kind enough to let me stage a show of his work. Your newspaper said his work was infantile and derivative. A man named Sanford, as I recall."

"He's the art critic. That was his opinion."

"He's a liar, and that was a scandalous piece of libel. You journalists are all alike—you tear down those you can't understand. That's why I've told my family to have nothing to do—"

"I'm not here as a journalist," I said.

She gave me a Circe look. I wanted to feel my nose to make sure it wasn't turning into a snout.

"More lies," she said.

This is what I get, I thought, for trying rudeness as a tactic. Like the young gunslinger, I had run into the champ. There was nothing to do but keep shooting.

"I'm here as a friend of your daughter-in-law."

Lucille, who had been so rich-bitch and superior when she'd first let me in, had faded and lost focus in Alma's presence, like the image on a movie screen in a bright light. When I saw the look the older woman turned on her now, I almost expected her to wink out of existence altogether.

She didn't, though. She met the gaze, and said, "Not me, Mother."

The cold eyes swung back to me. I figured the least I could do was be as brave as Lucille. "No," I said. "Not her. I should have said I'm a friend of your stepdaughter-in-law."

The eyes were no longer cold. In front flash, they melted and burned. "Get out of my house!"

"She did marry your stepson, didn't she?"

"Get out, or I'll have Louis throw you out!"

I looked at Louis, then showed him a little smile. I discovered that smile back in high school. Look amused enough, and you'll never have to find out if you are actually as tough as you think you are. Louis did not seem especially enthusiastic at the idea of throwing me out.

"She does have rights," I told the old woman. It was hard to meet that glare more than a few seconds. "The baby—your late husband's grandchild—has rights."

"That child is nothing to Andrew Letron! And that little tramp has no right to try to fob off her despicable little bastard as Paul's son. It will not be tolerated. It . . . will . . . not . . . be . . . *tolerated!*"

The heat vanished as quickly as it came. She was all ice again. She looked at me, as though wondering why she'd wasted so much energy on me. "Do you speak to the creature?"

I wanted to do a little exploding of my own, but I was controlling myself. "Yes," I said.

"Tell her, then. Tell her. No matter how many lawyers she bribes, how many corrupt men, French or American, she gets to help her with her big brown eyes and her little-girl innocence. She will not get away with it. I'll see her dead first."

From Lucille, there was something between a gasp and a groan. From Louis, there was a strangled, "Mother."

Alma ignored them both. "You'll tell her?" she demanded.

I shook my head. "She already knows."

I listened to myself say that, decided life only gives you a certain number of perfect exit lines, and decided to take it. For all my worrying though, it turned out to be harder to get out of that room than it had been to get in it. First Alma tromped all over my exit by sniffing loudly and getting up from her throne and gliding from the room. Then Louis and Lucille surrounded me and started telling me, pleading almost, that Mother Didn't Really Mean It. I said of course, and kept trying to make it out the door.

Lucille at one point even took me by the hand and asked me to understand. I remember being surprised that such a cool-looking blonde would have such warm hands. Then I got another surprise, but before I could do anything about it, I was at the door. I grabbed the knob, said a hasty good-bye, and left.

But the Letron family wasn't done with me yet. As the elevator doors were closing, just before they met, a tall, slim young man slithered between them and grinned at me triumphantly.

I knew he was a Letron (Peter, twenty-two, the youngest one) for two reasons. One, he had the look, and two, the hotel wouldn't let a maintenance man dress so shabbily. Peter was wearing green twill work pants and a white T-shirt under a plaid flannel lumberjack shirt. All were sweat-stained and perforated with dozens of brown-edged holes. Like he'd been blasted by a shotgun, or was the sloppiest smoker in the world.

He followed my eyes and read my mind. "I work in these clothes. Welded sculpture. Glass blowing. Car customizing."

"You're Peter," I informed him. "Faith told me about you." She'd told me that of all the Letrons, Peter had been the least troublesome, because he spent so much time at his hobbies, he had no time for anything else.

"I figured. Listen, I heard you talking to the clan back there."

"You and your mother both."

"Listening at keyholes is a family trait. The difference is, I admit it."

"So you listened. You want to tell me I've got it all wrong, too?"

He stopped grinning. "No, I just *hope* you've got it all wrong. Weird stuff is going on, and I'm worried."

"Like to tell me about it?"

"Yeah, but not now."

"Why not?"

"I can't get out of the elevator. I shouldn't even be out in the corridor. If the hotel people see me in these clothes, they'll know I've been torching in the suite again."

"Torching?"

"Propane, you know. A small one. Nothing dangerous. I'm doing some glass sculpture—I could go nuts from boredom in this place."

"And the hotel management doesn't want you to do it."

"Right," he said. The injustice of it all was bothering him. "All because I set fire to their lousy curtain once. I put the fire out. We paid for the curtain."

I fought down an urge to storm out of the building. I figured if he was with me, he couldn't be burning the place down. I didn't want to know if I was wrong.

"So when are you going to tell me all about it?" Whatever it was. I was losing track.

"How about tonight? Eight o'clock okay?"

"Sure," I said. I was about to ask where we should meet. Instead, I said, "I mean, no. How about tomorrow afternoon? Say four o'clock. Do you know where The Grayness building is?"

"I'll find it," he said.

"Good," I said. The elevator arrived in the lobby. Peter hid in the corner until the door closed, and the machine took him back up. I noticed all this without really paying attention. All my attention was devoted to the little piece of Westbrook Hotel stationery Lucille had surprised me with; her warm hands pressed it into mine just before I'd left the suite.

I hadn't been able to wait anymore, and I sneaked a look at it while Peter and I were talking. It had the name and address of a small French restaurant. It would be French. The rest of it read, "Tonight. Eight o'clock. Please be there. Must talk to you. L."

I'd be there all right. It was beginning to look as if secret assignations were another family trait.

CHAPTER THIRTEEN

I went back to The Grayness before I went home. It was out of the way, at right angles to my apartment, in fact, but I was hoping for some results from my overseas phone calls.

What I had done was to bend the journalistic mechanisms of The Grayness to my own ends. The foreign bureaus (especially the big ones, like the one in Paris) are pretty much at the beck and call of anyone in New York who can think of a decent excuse, or even a feeble one. Mine was that someone on the TV page had asked me to gather research on the Ten Best Real-Life Stories That Have Yet To Be Made Into TV Docudramas, and that Paul Letron would be mentioned, because there were so many rumors about him and so few facts. Rumors always make better docudramas than facts.

Anyway, the Paris people had to fall for it. I had told them to send anything they got to my desk at The Grayness. They probably would have gotten suspicious if I'd asked them to send the stuff to my apartment.

The best I expected to find on my desk was a phone message, maybe a Telex. What I got was a huge package of wire-facsimiles. I was costing The Grayness a lot of money on this. I felt guilty, but I could stand it. It was not hard to assuage my conscience with the idea that there really could be a story in this mess.

It was getting harder and harder to doubt Faith's story. There was the marriage certificate. Two of them, actually. Church and civil. In France, apparently, you need both. There was a certified copy of the will Paul Letron had made. I hadn't practiced my French since the famous semester abroad, but as far as I could make out, it tallied with Faith's account in every particular.

It occurred to me that it was a little odd for a lawyer to hand out a copy of the will like that, on the basis of one secondhand request from an American reporter. I didn't (and don't) know anything about French law, but hell, the client wasn't even actually dead yet.

The next document answered my question. I mean, it was still odd, but at least I knew why the lawyer had felt free to send the will along. The next thing in the pile was a fax of a certified copy of the signed instructions Letron had filed with him, authorizing him to cooperate with anyone authorized by his wife to see any document whatever, up to and including the will. He must have foreseen that people would be a little put out with all these unorthodox arrangements.

There was also a document designed to take care of the issue of artificial insemination. It stated that the undersigned, Paul Letron, a resident of the Republic of France and a citizen of the United States of America, and so on and so forth, had frozen a quantity of his sperm, and had left it in the care of the clinic herein described, and the doctor so named, and hereby authorized his wife, Faith, access to it at her sole discretion. It went on to state in no uncertain terms that he, and he alone, was to be considered the father of any child said wife might conceive from the date of the signing of this document until such time, if any, that she remarry. Furthermore, the document passed everything to the kid as soon as he (or she) was born if Letron had not yet died by then.

I wouldn't have thought it was possible a few minutes ago, but I was beginning to be a little sorry for Alma Letron. She could rant and rave all she wanted to about "We will not allow it," but the way her stepson had set things up, that kid could come out *Chinese*, and the family wouldn't be able to challenge its paternity.

For the first time, I was beginning to think that maybe somebody *was* out to murder Faith.

I immediately told myself not to be ridiculous. This was a

fascinating situation, and there were some strange personalities involved, Faith's among them. But murder conspiracies, I mean, come on. The situation was melodramatic enough without murder. Granted, it happens sometimes, these bizarre and terrible murder cases, rich people, weird motives, actual doubt about the guilt of the accused. Usually, they happen in Texas. Reporters cover them, and lap them up in their greedy, gossip-loving little hearts, before regurgitating them like mother seagulls for a public piping up for excitement. Undoubtedly, at this moment, sixteen top reporters are waiting for two more rich people in Texas to get together as murderer and victim so they can swoop in, write a book about it, and make a lot of money.

But in this case, the theoretical victim-to-be was a friend of mine, someone I had known literally since she was in diapers. Furthermore, I, as the folks at The Grayness kept me constantly aware, was not a Real Reporter. Therefore, this could not be a Real, or even a Potentially Real, murder case.

It was, however, a Real Case of galloping paranoia in progress when I returned to my apartment.

For one thing, it took me four minutes to convince my own sister to take the chain bolt off the door to my own apartment. For another, I did not get the sort of welcome an amateur detective deserved after a busy and progress-filled day of sleuthing.

"About time you got back," Sue said. She sounded exhausted.

"I'm going out again," I said. "Have to take a shower and change."

"You're going back to *them,*" Faith said. Sue had found her a flannel nightgown somewhere that almost fit. She made it sound as if I were going out to eat with James Arness and a bunch of giant ants.

"I'm looking into things. I'm getting to the bottom of it. The more I learn, the more I believe you."

"You don't believe they want to kill me. Kill my baby."

I took a deep breath. "Let me put it this way. From what I've learned today, I believe that if they want what you say they want, then what you say they want to do is what they're going to have to do if they want to get it."

Sue said, "Huh?"

Faith either got it, or she had something more important on her mind. "I wasn't *thinking,*" she moaned. "I should never have talked to you on the phone this afternoon."

"Why not?"

"You know why not."

"She's been like this all day," Sue said.

Faith deigned to tell me why not. As soon as my phone call was over, Faith had decided my mission had been a bad idea. What *good* could it do? All I was likely to have accomplished was to warn Them (and the capital was plain in her voice) that Faith had found allies. I had only put myself, and Sue, in danger.

I looked at her. Since I had met Alma, I had to take the danger more seriously. I was kicking myself for not having seen this possibility. I said as much.

"Of course you didn't see it." Faith could be magnanimous now that I'd conceded she was right. "I know how hard this is to believe. But I've been living with this for months now—it . . . does something to your mind."

And there we were, I thought, right back to the entrance to this particular amusement park.

"And it won't make any difference," Faith went on. Her voice held gloom worthy of a hard-boiled Los Angeles private eye. "They've gone too far now to be scared off. There's too much at stake for them to quit. They have to kill me, or at least make me have a miscarriage, and all this is going to do is make them more determined and more cautious about how they go about it."

Sue made the kind of noise in her throat people make when they're about to say something they think is going to embarrass them.

Faith didn't let her get it out. "Really," she insisted. "All I need is a safe place to stay until the baby comes. It should only be a couple of weeks. Once the baby is born, they can't do anything—if anything happens to the child, the money goes to charity, and they lose it forever. I'll be safe. Paul's baby will be safe. It's all I need, really. Can't you arrange for some quiet out-of-the-way place for me? Where they won't find me? I'd just like my baby to be born in peace."

Still favoring her injured left hand, Faith walked clumsily around my living room looking for the ratty canvas shoulder bag she'd had when she arrived. "I'm not going to freeload on anybody. Where's my bag? I can pay, you know. I'll show you."

"I know you can pay," I said. After those documents this afternoon, boy, did I know. "Don't insult our friendship by offering me money. You can stay here. If you don't think it's safe here, you can go to Scarsdale and stay with my mother. Or, if you don't mind getting official about things, I'll find out where The Grayness stows sources and wangle you into there. I admit, I'm going to have the doorman be extra careful about who comes into this building. And I'll stay here tonight myself."

"Oh," Faith said. "You don't have to do that. I mean, Lucille is a bitch, but she's shrewd. Now that she knows I've told somebody responsible what's going on, and that you believe me, she might get the rest of them to listen to reason."

"Faith," I said, "a minute ago, nothing I did would make any difference. Which is it?"

Faith looked miserable. I felt like a louse.

"I don't *know,*" she said. "You make me feel better sometimes, but I'm afraid to feel better. I'm afraid to hope."

Sue made the noise again. This time, she got to talk. "Okay," she said. "Look, Faith. I know you're worried. If I were pregnant, and I even *suspected* I might be in a situation like yours, I don't know what I'd do. I'd probably shoot everybody who looked at me cross-eyed."

Faith grinned without humor. "Where do I get a gun?"

"Just think about this. If, as I do, I believe you're right about what's happening to you, I have to believe your in-laws have committed at least attempted murder, for God's sake. You've been to the police, the police don't believe you, okay. You were smart to come to Harry. Something like that has got to be checked out. Who knows what they may get up to next? Right, Harry?"

"Huh?" I said. I was goggling at my baby sister. Inspirational speeches from the girl who was upset at the man who shot the Pope because it cut into "As the World Turns." "Oh," I said. "Right. Absolutely."

"But still—"

"No, Faith," I said. "There are eight million people in New York, any one of them a potential innocent bystander. And if you want to say to hell with the innocent bystanders, I'm not sure I blame you. It's not that easy to find innocent people standing by. But think of yourself. Won't you feel better when this is all settled?"

"Oh, God," she said.

And that was it. I wasn't sure what I had convinced her of, or if I had wanted to, or if I was even the one who had convinced her. All I knew was, if I had just been hired to be a private eye, I'd better get moving if I expected to get to that restaurant in time to meet the suspect.

CHAPTER FOURTEEN

The place was called Le Cassoulet, a pretty unpretentious name, as names for French restaurants go. It was on Second Avenue in the Fifties, nestled unobtrusively into the ground floor of a five-story walkup. The front was a little shabby, the small window covered with more than a day's worth of city grime. The menu in the window was starting to yellow with age. The prices seemed a little low. They'd only been changed with ballpoint once during the life of this menu—par for one this old was three times.

I knew why. The restaurant was living on borrowed time, going through the motions until somebody got around to knocking down the walkup and putting up another fifty-story office building. The day is coming when the only building in New York between Fourteenth Street and Central Park under thirty stories tall will be St. Patrick's Cathedral.

The door made a cowbell ring when I pushed it open. That was probably the only way they could tell if someone had come in, since they appeared to be trying to save on electricity what they lost by not raising the prices. As far as I could tell in the gloom, the place was empty. That was to be expected. In that neighborhood, the pattern is a large crowd between five and seven, with people sneaking drinks before they head home or catching an early dinner before going out, then another wave around ten, when the movies and plays begin to let out.

A dark-haired young woman in the standard New York restaurant-hostess uniform of white blouse and floor-length gray skirt smiled at me and handed me a menu the size of a road map. I told her I was meeting someone. She asked me if I would like to wait at the bar.

By now, my eyes had adjusted to the darkness, and I could see the place wasn't deserted. There was a yellowish glow from a blond head, and the ghostly flash of a waved white hand. "Never mind," I said. "She's already here."

The hostess smiled at me again, took the menu back and led me with Helen Keller-like ease through the darkness to the rear corner table Lucille Letron had chosen.

Lucille had a smile and a warm handshake for me, as well as another menu. There was a tiny candle in a red glass globe on the table, casting shadows on her face from below. It made her look slightly devilish, which I supposed was appropriate, at least from the point of view of one of Faith's faction. The red glow of the candle, however, also removed the coolness I had seen in her beauty earlier. I was going to have to watch myself.

"I'm glad you came," she said. "Have you eaten?"

Neither of us had. I opened the menu and squinted. The handwriting was old and faded. A waiter came by, a young man with curly hair and big soulful eyes. "Would you like anything from the bar?"

Lucille asked for a Campari and soda. I settled for just the soda. The level of health consciousness in New York has at last risen to such a point that you can refrain from alcohol in a restaurant without being looked upon as a carrier of typhus. I might have gone down in the history (soon to be concluded) of Le Cassoulet as a totally run-of-the-mill customer, but I had another request.

"Might we have another candle please?"

"Excuse me?"

"I'd like another candle."

He pointed. The tip of his index finger became visible in the weak red glow that extended three inches beyond the glass. "What's wrong with this one?"

"Nothing's wrong with that one," I said. "I said I wanted another one, not a different one. I need more light so I can read the menu."

"I see, sir." He reached over to the next table, grabbed another candle and plunked it down next to the first one.

"Thanks," I said. Lucille, who had suppressed gasps all afternoon, was now suppressing giggles. The waiter said he'd go get our drinks now and walked off.

Lucille was now lit from below by two candles. It made her look more devilish than ever. More attractive, too. The giggles hadn't hurt. She was rapidly becoming human.

"You like to stir people up," she said. "Don't you?"

"Not especially," I said. I squinted again at the menu, then picked up one of the candles and held it between me and the cardboard. "I should have asked for a flashlight. You must have good eyes. How's the food here? Have you eaten here before?"

"Frequently," she said. There was a flash in her eyes, as if there were something amusing about that.

The waiter came back with our drinks and took our order. I decided to make it easy and take the restaurant's word for what they did well, and ordered the cassoulet. Lucille ordered *magret de canard*, rare.

"I'm glad this isn't a nouvelle cuisine place," I said. "I mean, I was willing to meet you any place you liked, but now I won't have to stop at McDonald's afterward."

"No," she said. "I don't think you'll want anything else. A person can live on one serving of their cassoulet for days at a time."

"That's good. Nouvelle cuisine tastes all right, usually, but I could never really consider three ounces of pheasant, eighteen grains of rice, and two green grapes a meal."

We talked about French food until our own French food came. The cassoulet was terrific. The beans were big and soft, and the sausages and hunks of lamb and pork were as good as anything I'd had in France. *Magret de canard* is supposed to be the meat sliced off the breast of a duck grilled like a steak, but from the slab on Lucille's plate, they had used a swan at least. Maybe a roc. We wished each other good appetite, then dug in.

I ate three days' worth of cassoulet, and Lucille did honor to her duck, or whatever. She still hadn't raised the subject she supposedly wanted to talk to me about. I mentioned it.

"Oh," she said, shrugging it off. "It isn't so much that I wanted

to talk to you. Though I will, off the record." She looked the
question at me; I nodded. "What I really want is to show you
something. Possibly. Depending how dinner goes."

"Good," I said. "A man needs something to live up to. I
thought we were going to discuss Faith." I could never say that
without feeling like a TV evangelist.

"I suppose the subject will come up."

"Consider it up already. What are you going to do about your
mother-in-law?"

Lucille had obviously decided that the attitude for this eve-
ning would be "unconcerned." "She is a problem. Definitely
around the bend. Faith would be in real danger, if anyone
listened to the old witch."

"You looked and acted as if you were listening to her."

"I was listening to the impression she made on *you*. With
dread, believe me. When she tells Robert to instruct the corporation not to pay any taxes this year, because they didn't do as
she asked in a hundred letters (which we never mail) and forbid
the importation of foreign cosmetics, we don't listen. When she
tells us to instruct the hotel to clear the floors directly above and
below ours so we won't be disturbed, we don't listen."

"Your husband is running the company now, I take it."

Lucille smiled. "Robert is such a dear."

"What does that mean?"

"It means that Robert makes a wonderful figure as president
of Letronique. He's handsome, and he makes a great speech.
But he'll never be a businessman."

"The company's still healthy. Momentum from Paul?"

"Mostly. That and the fact that no one knows how sick Paul is.
Robert is smart enough to know that Paul built a top-notch
management team, and to take their advice on everything. Still,
once Paul dies—did she tell you it's supposed to be any minute?"

"I heard. You don't seem especially broken up about it."

"I was. I had been, until Faith—you see, I told you she'd come
up. Until Faith went to her Dr. Frankenstein, and had that little
monster implanted in her."

"There's nothing wrong with artificial insemination. Especially in a situation like this. Paul wanted a child. This is the only way."

"Call me superstitious, then."

"What's the matter? Don't you think the baby is going to have a soul?"

"The whole thing just makes me ill. Can we talk about something else?"

"Sure," I said. I left a mental bookmark at the matter making her ill, though. If she felt strongly enough about soulless monster babies, it might be enough to encourage her to try to do something about it. Especially with the money thrown in as added incentive. "What happens when Paul dies?"

"Excuse me?"

"The last thing you said before we got sidetracked was, 'Once Paul dies . . .'"

"Oh. I was talking about the executives at the company. Once it comes out how sick Paul is, people will realize that it's the management team that's been running the company for the last few years, and they'll be hired away. I keep telling Robert the best thing to do is to have them look around for a merger. Then even with Faith's little experiment, we should be fine."

"Faith seems to think you'll have more money in any case than any rational person needs."

"You've met us. You've met Alma. What makes you think you're talking to rational people?"

I didn't say anything.

"That settles it," she said. She waved for the check. She wanted to pay, but I was damned if I was going to let a millionairess buy me dinner. A stupid notion, when you come to think of it, but I was stuck with it. I whipped out my American Express card (feeling slightly ashamed it was only a green one—the Letrons undoubtedly carried gold cards at least), and it was snapped up by the waiter before she could protest.

"All right," she said. "Pretend to be proud. You'll learn it doesn't make any difference."

I didn't even try to figure out what she meant by that. The

credit slip returned. I added and signed and removed carbons. I kept the counterfoil—this could turn into a deductible business expense, yet. The Grayness would laugh in my face if I ever tried to turn in an expense account to them.

"All done?" Lucille said. "Good. Come with me."

"Sure," I said. It was still early, and I had asked the doorman and a few of my more friendly neighbors to keep watch over Faith and Sue, so I wasn't too worried on that score. And I still wanted to get my money's worth from Lucille—I'd learned about a good, cheap French restaurant, and I'd learned some stuff about the family business I could have figured out for myself if I'd taken five minutes to think about it. I'd hang around for a while yet.

"Where are we going?"

"Not far," she said, as we emerged into the cool November air and the relative brightness of sodium vapor lamps on the avenue. "No distance at all, in fact."

Her voice sounded wistful; I looked at her face, and that was wistful, too. It was about the last sort of mood I'd ever have expected to see her in.

"Think of it," she said, "as a sort of time travel."

CHAPTER FIFTEEN

She let me stand out on the sidewalk for maybe five seconds before she turned around and walked back to the building.

"What's the matter?" I asked. "Forget something inside?"

But she didn't go back into the restaurant, she walked into the doorway right next to it, the one that led upstairs to the apartments. She looked back over her shoulder at me. "Come on," she said. "I told you I've decided to show you something."

"Like what? Housebreaking techniques?"

For someone who felt like an outcast at the newspaper I worked for, it was amazing how many real-reporter-type attitudes I had managed to pick up. Journalistic paranoia, for instance. A setup, that's what this had to be. She'd get me into somebody's apartment, hit me on the head, leave me, call the cops, get me arrested . . .

"Are you coming or not?"

Who dares wins, I thought. "Sure."

There was no ambush waiting in the hallway. Lucille had her keys out. She opened a mailbox that a peeling Dymo label said belonged to "L. Burke." There was no mail inside, but there was a three-inch stack of those little bookmark-shaped things locksmiths and exterminators in New York spend their idle time slipping through mailbox slots.

Another key opened the inner door. Lucille let me up two flights of stairs through a shabby but clean hallway to third floor front—L. Burke's apartment. She had keys to that one, too.

I asked if L. Burke was expecting us.

"She knows we're coming." Lucille used keys: a Fichet on the top lock, a Rabson on the bottom, a Medeco on the one in the middle.

That was a good three hundred dollars' worth of locks. Nobody could be that protective of merely her life. "What does she keep in here? The Crown Jewels?" Lucille chuckled, the first time I'd heard her do that.

It was a studio apartment, standard New York issue for buildings of that vintage. Room, about twelve by eighteen, kitchen (stove, the bottom half of a refrigerator, sink), and a bathroom. One window, fronting the street, ancient air conditioner stuck into the wall under half of it, heating register under the other half. An apartment like this now costs about seven hundred dollars a month to rent, depending on the neighborhood.

"How do you like it?" Lucille said. She sounded like someone who's just given you a birthday present.

I looked around. When you live in a studio apartment, you have a choice. You can have a living room (condemning yourself to a lifetime of sleeping on one of those wretched fold-out sofas), or you can have a bedroom, leaving yourself open to misinterpretation every time you have somebody visit. This place was a bedroom. A good portion of the twelve by eighteen was taken up with a double-sized bed in white pine, with a quilted white spread. There were matching bedside tables, with plain white lamps on them. The carpet, where it was visible, was blue, one of the plush carpets that were so big in the seventies, the kind with no discernible pile, just an undifferentiated sea of fuzz.

Not much of the carpet was visible—the rest of the place looked like somebody's attic. There were trunks, in various stages of decrepitude, with the occasional sleeve or piece of frill sticking out from the crack of a closed lid. No bookshelves, but piles of books, tottering structures of indiscriminately mixed hardcovers and paperbacks that looked as if they'd fall over at the first puff of air. Stacks of magazines, too. *Vogue, Cosmopolitan,* The Grayness *Sunday Magazine.* Scrapbooks. There were stuffed animals and dolls. There were little pieces of porcelain covered in dust (the whole place was dusty; no one had been in here in weeks) and set down on any available surface. There were records, albums and singles, but nothing to play them on.

I turned to Lucille. "I love it," I said. "I lived in one of the clones of this place my first two years in New York."

"So did I."

"The decor was different, though. I had comic books strewn all over the—"

She was laughing. I spent a good part of the day in this woman's presence, and she'd been gasping and smiling and frowning and giggling and chuckling, but this was the first display of emotion from her I was willing to bet was genuine.

Now was the time to say something brilliant. I did not rise to the occasion. "You're L. Burke," I said.

She nodded. "I was. For a while. Before I was Lucille Letron. After," she added, "I got tired of being Lucille Berkowitz."

This was not my night to shine. I responded to this with four words I thought I'd never say. "You don't look Jewish."

She pointed to the pile of scrapbooks. "Go take a look at my old nose," she said. "This one's only about six years old."

I looked. I don't know why I wasn't willing to take her word for it. The first thing I opened to was a clipping with the headline *Area Students in Dance Recital,* and there was little Lucille Berkowitz, one of the soloists, executing a jeté, her old nose cleaving the air ahead of her. A few pages later, there was a front-page headline that said: HIGH SCHOOL JUNIOR WINS NATIONAL SCIENCE PRIZE. There was a picture of her with an award. There were lots more clippings. Not all of them had pictures, but there was plenty of evidence.

Yes, I thought, this is the reason there are no poor plastic surgeons. Old noses make the difference. Here I'd been figuring her for Superwasp, and she turned out to be another Westchester Jew. Just like me. The only differences were, I still had my old nose, and my name job had been performed before I had a chance to do anything about it.

"You have me at your mercy, you know," she said.

I told her I didn't see how.

"They don't know."

"Who doesn't know about what?"

"The family doesn't know about this apartment. Doesn't

know about my past. You could destroy them if you told on me. Especially if you told Alma. She almost disowned Robert for marrying me because she thinks I'm Protestant. The Letrons are old French stock, you know. Staunch Catholics. She might have succeeded in getting it called off if Paul didn't put his foot down. Paul was—is—a hell of a nice guy. The family knows how messed up they're going to be without him."

"Bully for them," I said. "How did you bring it off? What did you tell your parents?"

She shrugged. "Nothing. By the time I was out of college, I'd lost touch with them, anyway. My parents were the children of business partners who got married because their fathers said they should, and they weren't really into it, if you know what I mean. They were divorced when I was ten. I don't know where my father is. My mother stuck it out until I was safely into Smith, then took off to San Francisco to come out of the closet."

She looked at me. "Not 'The Goldbergs,' is it?"

"What did you tell the Letrons?"

"I told them I was an orphan. I was working for Austin Stoddard & Trapp as an assistant editor when I met Robert in the bar of the Westbrook."

"That's practically a cliché," I said.

She nodded soberly. "It is, isn't it? Out of Smith, into publishing; it's practically required."

"You told him you were an orphan."

"I might as well be. My mother sends a birthday card here every September, and I send her one back in February, if I remember. This place comes in handy as a mail drop. I pay for it out of my allowance. Robert thinks I spend all that money getting my hair done." She said it as though it were an endearing trait of Robert's. As if she wanted to tack the phrase "the big lug" onto the end of the sentence, but didn't because she was too used to talking to classy people. "I don't know what I'm going to do when they tear the building down."

"You could rent a post office box for five dollars a month," I told her.

"Yes, but when I took up with Robert, when I met Alma, I

knew I'd have to leave little Lucille Berkowitz behind. Lucille Burke was close to her, just cosmetic changes, really, a better name, a better nose. Lucille Letron couldn't have anything to do with little Miss Berkowitz. Do you understand?"

"Not entirely."

"Look. I *liked* little Lucille. She had a basically miserable childhood, but she was an achiever, she did a lot of neat stuff for an unwanted little girl with a big nose. She taught Lucille Burke how to get what she wanted, and Ms. Burke did. I just don't want to lose complete touch with the kid, you know?"

"And yet you risk it all," I said.

"What do you mean?"

"As you said, you're at my mercy. I could walk out of here, make one phone call and end it all for you."

"After all this time, I don't think Robert would mind. Alma would want to kill me, but Robert and I are habits with each other. He knows I like to spend money, and I know he likes to stand out in the woods chopping things while mosquitoes bite him. He takes care of me when I get too neurotic, and I soothe him and go fetch his ampoule when his angina acts up. So I think we'd survive this."

"It wouldn't be pleasant," I said.

"No."

"It would be very inconvenient."

"Yes."

"Then why tell me?"

"Because I want you to understand. About Faith. I figured you would be the one to tell. *I* would talk to *you* about Faith, and you would understand."

"Why?"

Her lovely Wasp face said she couldn't believe it. "Because we're *all alike*, can't you see? Middle-class kids from middle-class lives, trying to get to the top of something. You with your glamorous career with a powerful newspaper. Faith and I marrying money. Faith just did a better job of it than I did."

"A better job."

"Can you blame me for resenting her? I made myself over,

and stored my past in a little walkup to get close to the Letrons. I tried to be what they thought they wanted, especially what Robert and his mother wanted. Nouveaux riches are always the worst snobs, so I gave them blond and Waspy, and despite all the non-Catholic business, they loved it.

"But Faith. Faith just had to be her own sweet, helpless, pitiful little self. And she not only got everything I'd gotten, she got the best brother, as well. Of course I resent her."

"You wanted Paul."

"The minute I met him. He had the money, he had the power, he had the brains. Unfortunately, I had already let Robert make me pregnant by then."

"You have a child?" Faith had never mentioned it.

"Miscarriage, thank God. With my luck, the little monster would have had my old nose, and everyone would have wondered where it came from. And he would have been an unnatural, poisonous wretch, like his grandmother. Like both his grandmothers."

She moved a little closer to me. I could smell perfume, faint, but spicy-sweet. "I wanted you to understand, Harry. We're all alike, you, me and Faith. I wanted you to understand."

"I'm not like you," I said.

"But you like me."

"I don't like you."

"But you want me." She touched my cheek. It burned.

I should have resisted her, I suppose. But this woman had gotten under my skin the first instant I saw her, and somehow, learning she was not the embodiment of my Wasp fantasies after all (she was the embodiment of *her* Wasp fantasies), only made it worse. Besides, since the Great Heartbreak of my life ten months ago, I had not touched or kissed a woman I wasn't a blood relative of, and if you don't think that makes a difference, you are more than human, or less, and God bless you.

So we kissed and undressed and climbed on the bed. Mrs. Letron knew what she wanted, and she knew what I wanted, and she was not shy about asking or giving. All around us was the presence of little Lucille Berkowitz, something I felt especially strongly at those moments the woman with me gave a shriek, or a dirty little laugh. At those moments, it felt like more than a tumble with a beautiful but irritating married woman. It was almost like an exorcism, or a sacrifice.

It ended. It always does. Lucille wanted me to stay, but I had a vision of Faith and Sue's expressions when I walked in in the morning after staying away all night, and said I couldn't.

Lucille sighed. "All right. We must do it again sometime." She had that smug smile on her face, the one women get when they think they've put one over on you and made you like it. She sat naked on the bed and watched me as I dressed. There was no need for me to wear a tie now. Tying it just gave me something to concentrate on, so I wouldn't have to answer her.

Lucille got off the bed and pressed her tall body against my suit and gave me a long slow kiss before I left. She seemed satisfied, which is what a man with sufficiently raised consciousness is always hoping to see. I was satisfied.

I hoped Lucille's demons were.

CHAPTER SIXTEEN

I met with Peter Letron the next day, but a lot earlier than originally planned, and in a different place, and for a different reason.

The day started calmly enough, over bowls of farina for breakfast. I'm not a hot-cereal fan, but that stuff was terrific. Sue cooked it. I'd never seen her or heard of her cooking anything before, and I had a big-brother flash of suspicion—what's my baby sister been doing in college, getting all this practice at cooking breakfast? I was a fine one to talk, after last night.

Thinking about last night made me realize that what I was experiencing right now might be a certain amount of little-sister suspicion. I thought I'd just been lucky to avoid questions. The girls had been asleep when I got back last night, or they'd pretended to be. And this morning, there hadn't been a word about Lucille Letron. That just wasn't natural. If I was one of those people whose brain awakes at the same time their bodies do, I would have seen it a lot sooner.

That made *me* feel compelled to talk about it. I said I had a nice dinner, that we'd spoken about the financial and other aspects of the situation from both points of view, and that Lucille seemed to be on the level, but I was buying nothing from her without a lengthy test drive.

"One thing that occurred to me," I went on, "is that you could probably win Lucille over."

Faith stopped with the spoon halfway to her mouth. Milk and grains of farina made little splashes as they fell back into the bowl. It's hard for a pregnant woman to be haughty in a huge terry-cloth robe, while she's splashing milk around the table, but Faith managed it. "Why should I want to win that woman over?"

"I didn't say you should want to, I said you probably could. If you did want to."

"How?"

"How do you feel about the company? Is it a heritage you want your child to have? I mean, is it going to matter to you if the kid would rather be a nursery school teacher than a cosmetics tycoon?"

"Of course not. Children should do whatever they want."

That was encouraging. I told her Lucille's fears about Robert running the company into the ground, and her fears that Faith, as chief trustee (another little fact from the French facsimiles), would let him, or that she would boot Robert out altogether, and possibly hire somebody worse.

"That's none of her business!"

"I know. For God's sake, Faith, what did you want when you came to me? A preemptive guerrilla strike on your husband's family? Napalm? Neutron bombs?"

"That's what they're trying to do to me."

"It's possible. It's maybe even likely. I would not be flabbergasted to learn that the old lady has been spreading a little money around to people who hurt people for money."

"I'm sure she has."

"All right. It's going to be difficult to do anything about her without some help from inside the family. Since I personally am not into killing people . . ." I gave Faith a chance to say she wasn't either, but she neglected to take advantage of it. ". . . And I don't have enough money to hire somebody . . ." The idea that Faith did have enough crossed my mind, but I put it aside as unworthy. ". . . What needs to be done is to get her put away. And you can't do that without help from the family."

"I don't need their help. They're all in it."

I started to formulate a lecture to the effect that while paranoia in many circumstances was normal, and even healthy, sometimes, it was a great big pain in the ass. I decided to save it for a time when the audience would be more receptive.

"Look," I said. "I'll grant you they're worthless, all right?
They're drones, human parasites. But the key word here is
human. And humans worry about the future. *Especially* parasites and drones, because they're incapable of taking care of it
for themselves."

"My God," my sister said helpfully. "That almost makes
sense." Faith didn't say anything, but she was still looking at me,
ready to listen.

I made the most of it. I told her I wasn't trying to push her
into any position she didn't want to occupy, but that I felt
Lucille, and probably Peter and Louis, were plenty scared of
Alma themselves, and that they would all feel a lot better dis-
posed toward Faith if she made it clear she'd listen (on behalf of
the kid, of course) to merger offers from big companies, should
they come, and that she might even be willing to take the right
one, should *it* come. It was the longest sentence I've ever con-
structed.

Faith mumbled something. Sue begged her pardon.

"I'll *think* about it!" Faith said. She looked around, as if to see
who was yelling, then mumbled again, something about going
to get dressed.

Because today was a momentous occasion: we were Going
Out. All of us, Faith included. It was Sue's idea, but I went along
with it. Faith already felt as if she were under attack, but there
was no need for her to feel like a prisoner, too. Not that the trip
was scheduled to be especially strenuous. We were going down
to Lexington and Thirty-fourth Street to visit the gynecologist.

Dr. Barbara Metzenbaum was Sue's gynecologist, but Sue was
willing to lend her out for the duration of Faith's pregnancy.
Now, you may be wondering why a young woman who lives in
Scarsdale and attends college in Syracuse has a gynecologist in
Manhattan. All the Westchester coeds above a certain income
level do it. Why? To get diaphragms without their mothers'
finding out, is the big reason. The summer before they take off
for college is when it usually happens.

We knew from the folks at the hospital that Faith was healthy
as a horse, but there was still no doctor lined up to deliver the

baby. Sue didn't know if Dr. Metzenbaum did obstetrics as well
as diaphragm distribution, but even if she didn't, she'd be able
to refer Faith to someone who did.

No referrals were necessary. Dr. Metzenbaum apparently
delivered all the Yuppie babies on the East Side between Fifti-
eth Street and the Village, except those whose parents were
blood relatives of rival obstetricians.

The whole trip was very educational. I learned, for instance,
that a young man who walks into a gynecologist's waiting room
with two attractive young women of the same age, one of them
obviously pregnant, gets some funny looks from the other patients. Especially when the nurse summons and they *both* go in.
I thought of making a general announcement that one of them
was my sister, but that would only have made things worse.

Sue and Faith came out of the office smiling, which I took as a
sign of good news. I was all set to ask them for particulars when
the white-coated young woman stuck her head out the Dutch
door and said, "Mr. Ross? Would you come in here for a moment?"

I pointed to my chest. "Me?"

It was a stupid question, since I was the only man in the room,
but she answered it. "Mr. Harry Ross, yes." Then I really got
some funny looks.

I went inside, and she closed the top of the Dutch door with a
bang behind me. I jumped. "This way please."

I was led into a book-lined office, the kind they shoot TV
commercials in. There were framed diplomas on the wall (what
would a patient do if he ever walked into a doctor's office with
no framed diplomas on the wall? Leave? Insist on seeing them?)
announcing in Latin that Barbara Metzenbaum was hot stuff,
honors all over the place. I was glad that Faith was in such good
hands.

The whole place looked like money, which shouldn't have
been surprising, considering the whole neighborhood looked
like money. Something about living in New York, though,
makes you instantly classify as rich any store, office or home that
has a hundred square feet of bare carpet anywhere in it.

I expected to be invited to take a seat, to have a chance to be more fully impressed with the place while the nurse went off to find the doctor.

She didn't say anything. I found the silence a little uncomfortable, so I said something. "Nice office."

"I like it," the young woman said, and went behind the desk and sat down.

I expect the idea was for me to blurt out something like, "You're the *doctor?*" Fortunately, I was too busy thinking it to say it. Prosperous Murray Hill obstetrician/gynecologists should not look seventeen years old. They should be tall, striking brunettes who wear their hair in buns or twists, not petite strawberry blondes with their hair neck-length and parted (slightly crookedly) in the middle. They should be wearing some chic three-piece suit, or some kind of simple thing under a lab coat. They should not wear the lab coat over a madras shirt and tan corduroy trousers. They should not have freckles. They should not scorn makeup, and look incredibly cute without it.

They should not be mad at me.

"Mr. Ross, are you responsible for this?" If she were an M.D., she'd have to be about my age. Older, with an established practice like this. She looked like a teenager browned off at someone for reading her diary.

"For what?"

"You know perfectly well what."

I hate when people do that. This wasn't the time to make a point of it, however. "No, actually, my sister is behind it. Sue. She said you wouldn't mind—"

"Your sister can't be responsible for what I'm talking about, Mr. Ross."

"You think I—"

"Are you the father of that child?"

"Didn't they tell you anything?"

She looked at me with big brown eyes. Nice contrast with the hair. She shouldn't have been able to make me feel like she could thrash me within an inch of my life if she wanted to, but she did.

"They told me the most ridiculous story I've ever heard in my life."

"I agree."

That threw her off stride. "You admit it's a lie?"

"No, I agree it's ridiculous. I spent most of a day trying to prove it was false. I found out it was true, instead."

"Look, Mr. Ross. I have no objection to unmarried pregnancies . . ."

"I do."

". . . but if I'm going to do my best for an expectant mother, I have to have a medical history on the father, as well."

"I can see you get one," I told her. "That was part of the checking I did." I got a look at her face and said, "I don't expect you to believe me until you see it."

She smiled, even though she didn't want to. "That's good."

"Are you still going to treat Faith? I mean, if she goes into labor before I can get it to you?"

"Of course. And whether you're the father or not, I assume you care about her."

"She's a friend. Known each other since we were kids."

"Physically, she's in great shape. Emotionally . . ."

"Told you another weird story, didn't she?"

"Is this one true?"

"I don't know. The scary thing is, it might just be."

"Take care of her."

"Working on it. I'll get that report to you as soon as possible."

"That would be a help." She didn't say whether it would be a help medically, or in finding out if I was a liar.

"Would there be any objection if I brought it in person?"

"Why should there be?" she said. She started shuffling papers on her desk.

I left the office and joined the girls, then got a taxi for home. I spent most of the trip wondering if I'd been encouraged or not. I try never to ask a woman out until I'm sure she's going to say yes. There is something about me that makes being rejected feel like being the star attraction at a public disemboweling. The only trouble with my system is that it usually takes me six months to decide it's safe to ask, and by that time, she's usually married. Still, it was something to daydream about. At least she didn't say she'd puke if she saw me again. And my mother would be so pleased. Every Jewish mother wants her child to meet a nice doctor.

It was one of those rare days in New York—a day when the macadam in the street is actually visible between the cars, and the traffic actually moves. No one can explain why this happens. Does some mass benign instinct sweep through the suburbs and make the commuters decide to take the train that day? Have all the double-parked tractor-trailers made their deliveries the day before? Or does some freak atmospheric condition shrink each car an inch or two, thereby making several miles of new space? If you can figure it out, and learn how to produce the condition at will, not only will you be a billionaire, you will be the most beloved of New Yorkers since Fiorello La Guardia.

We stopped only for traffic lights, so instead of forty-five minutes to get crosstown four blocks and uptown forty-five, it took about twelve. That gives me time, I thought, to do a little thinking before I had to head over to The Grayness to meet Peter Letron.

Then Peter showed up, running full tilt from around the corner on York Avenue. Faith saw him first, and screamed. Peter was yelling something, but Faith, joined shortly by the usually unflappable Sue, drowned him out. They tried to crawl into my pocket. Failing that, they crouched down behind me.

I had to admit she had a point. Peter looked fairly maniacal. I told the girls to get inside. I stood my ground. I mean, I am not two-fisted death, or anything, but I was bigger than Peter was, and he didn't seem to have a gun or a knife, so what the hell.

Then I made out what he was yelling. *"No! Don't go inside! Don't go inside!"*

It occurred to me to yell back, "Why the hell not?" But that could wait until he got closer.

Just then, Sue came back out of the doorway. She was dragging Faith by the arm, but the only reason Faith wasn't in front was that she was slowed down by her bulk.

Sue was breathless. "It's a trap," she told me. "Louis is inside."

Peter was still running full tilt, but he had enough wind to continue to yell. I remembered he did glass blowing. *"It's a trap!"* he yelled. *"Louis is inside!"*

Faith looked at me, I looked at her. We both looked at Sue, we all looked at Peter. He was almost upon us, but we were now too bewildered to do anything but let him run.

CHAPTER SEVENTEEN

It had been a very small, very compact bomb. The doorman had a few cuts on his face, but he was healthy enough. He was calling the police as I went into the lobby to assess the damage. It was still the tacky-elegant combination of marble floors, foil wallpaper and fake tropical plants it had always been. There was no smoke, and no more smell than a hibachi makes. There was a mess on the floor, but it would have been just as bad a mess if someone had come back from D'Agostino's around the corner, slipped on the marble, fallen down and broken a bottle of cranberry juice.

So how come I wanted to throw up?

I devoted myself to fighting off the feeling. Eventually, my brain was able to get past the idea that it was in fact a dead body down there, and go to work on details. The hair. The face. The topcoat, at least the parts of it below the breastbone and above the navel, all of which had been relatively untouched by the explosion. Even the scarf. I recognized them all from yesterday. Louis Letron.

There were a few scraps of cardboard and brown paper around, something that added to the supermarket motif. A couple of large pieces of paper had landed writing up. One of them said, "by hand," and the other read "aith Le," and maybe more, but the rest was obscured by blood.

That settled that. I came out of my trance, and realized I had left my sister and Faith on the sidewalk with another of the dreaded Letron brothers. I ran back outside to deal with the crisis. This did not please the doorman, who had undoubtedly just been told by a desk sergeant not to let anyone leave the scene. He shouted something after me; I told him I'd be back.

There was no crisis, at least nothing that had to be dealt with immediately. The girls weren't ready for the Easter parade, but they weren't cowering in fear, either. Peter kept apologizing and explaining.

"I saw Louis leaving the suite as I was coming back—I'd been down to a hobby shop on Seventh Avenue for supplies—and while we were saying hello, I noticed the address on the package."

"Addressed to Faith?" I said.

He nodded. "To Faith in care of you. I was going to ask him about it, but I didn't. I didn't think it would do any good. First, he covered it up, the address, I mean, and when he saw I'd caught him at it, he smiled and said it was a peace offering." Peter cleared his throat.

A *piece* offering, I thought. To separate her and the baby into component pieces. Luck, in the form of defective materials or Louis's own incompetence, were the only things that kept it from happening. For the first time since all this started, Faith could have broken down into hysterics with my complete sympathy. Naturally, she didn't. She adopted an attitude best described as grim triumph.

"I told you," she said. "Didn't I say they were after me?"

"Faith," Peter said. "Not they. Honestly. I'm sick over this. To think that my own brother . . ." And then *he* had hysterics, and Faith (of all people) began to soothe him. Obviously she was getting in some there-there practice for impending motherhood.

Sue took me aside for a word. "Well, big brother," she said. "This removes the last of your doubts, doesn't it?"

I didn't even bother to laugh.

"What are we going to do now?" Sue wanted to know.

"I think we'd better tell the whole story to the police when they get here. And I'll be careful handling packages from here on in."

"I mean about Faith," she said.

"The cops are used to looking out for people. I am an amateur. If Peter hadn't shown up when he did; if Louis somehow hadn't set the bomb off himself, we all would have been dead."

"We can't abandon Faith now!"

"Hallelujah!"

"Making fun of me isn't going to help. Faith is on the brink of collapse, Harry, and if we walk away from her, she might lose the baby, or go nuts or something."

"She seems to be taking things really well, actually."

"You don't know her at all, do you? Sure she looks like she's taking it fine, now. That's because her brain is only letting her intellect know what's going on. When it filters through to her emotions, watch out."

"Thank you, Dr. Freud. I thought you were a geology major."

"Ha, ha. I thought you were a friend."

"Ha, ha yourself, twerp." She hates it when I call her twerp, "Anyway, who said anything about walking away from her? All I'm saying is we're going to be guided by what Faith wants us to do for her (she may not be too pleased with me, after this, you know), and what the cops let us do for her."

"Where are the cops?" Sue wanted to know. The answer came to her through the cool November breeze in the form of sirens.

I heard them, too, and I thought of how excited I used to be when I heard them as a kid. I'd be a reporter, I thought, and I'd follow those sirens to exciting and important events, and I'd tell everybody about it . . .

That's when I came down with a sudden attack of Dr. Journalist and Mr. Hide. Even as I was strolling the few yards to the phone booth, even as I identified myself to the city desk ("Harry *who?*"), even as I gave a report of the explosion (but not of the intrigue behind it—that could wait for a byline); in short, even as I functioned like a Real Reporter, I wanted to run away. I knew what kind of feast those vultures *(we* vultures?) would make out of a story like this, and I regretted it already.

CHAPTER EIGHTEEN

"The day after tomorrow is Thanksgiving," I said.

The detective was wearing a five-hundred-dollar, three-piece suit. He hooked his thumbs in the armholes of his vest like Lionel Barrymore and said, "So?"

It was a fair response, since it had had nothing to do with the question he'd asked in the first place, which had been something like, "You mean, this girl is your sister's best friend, and she disappears for three years, and here you are, a reporter for a big newspaper, with all this investigative machinery you could use, which you admit you eventually *did* use, to find out where she was and what she was up to, and you didn't?"

Maybe I made the Thanksgiving remark because I was thinking how much nicer it would be to be eating turkey and watching the Detroit Lions play football than it was to be answering questions like that one. Or perhaps it was supposed to be a subtle reminder to Detective Lieutenant Craig Rogers that if he kept asking questions with nine clauses in them, we'd still *be* here day after tomorrow.

"Here" was some godforsaken building in the East Nineties currently masquerading as the Nineteenth Precinct. The Nineteenth Precinct used to be located on a charming, unobtrusive, quiet, tree-lined block on East Sixty-seventh. To see a police precinct amid all that affluence was reassuring. It nurtured an illusion that here on the Upper East Side, crime was not only being fought, but defeated. No more—they had moved uptown, on the theory, I guess, that the police should be close to where the crime is. I forgot whether the move was supposed to be temporary or permanent, but either way, I didn't like it much, and the neighbors in the old location were going to like it even less. Now they'd have to come up into the shadow of Spanish Harlem to report they'd been burglarized, or robbed of their imported racing bicycles.

Craig Rogers didn't seem to like it much, either, but that was probably a side effect of the impression I got that he didn't like *anything* much. Except himself. He liked himself just fine. He had a habit of taking sidelong glances at the apple-green walls, as if he were checking to see if a mirror had grown there since the last time he looked. I concede he had every right to be pleased by what he might see if there had been a mirror.

I had never met Craig Rogers before, but I had heard of him. He was newsworthy. He was the City's youngest homicide lieutenant, and he had a spectacular record. His latest triumph had been an art-forgery murder scandal the previous summer, though he looked uncharacteristically sheepish when I mentioned it. "I had a lot of help on that one," he said.

If he didn't get so much ink and airtime for being good at his job, he might have found the amount of publicity he got for other reasons embarrassing. He was always turning up on lists of "handsomest" and "most eligible" bachelors in New York, and his name had even been seen occasionally in gossip columns, usually for showing up at a nightclub with a TV starlet on his arm.

Right now, though, he wanted to know about Thanksgiving.

"Nothing," I said. "I was just being wistful."

"Try being truthful."

This was the point where I should get indignant, or at least sarcastic. They did it in all the best private-eye movies.

I didn't. I just told him that truthful was all I ever wanted to be, and answered his question. Of course, I ignored the real point of the question—the suggestion that I did in fact find out about Faith ahead of time, and participated with the Letrons in some unspecified plan to do her dirty. I wasn't worried about it, since they'd find out what a lot of hot air it was when they spoke to Faith.

"I might have tried to do something about finding Faith"—it

was impossible to talk about her without sounding like the 700 Club—"if my sister had asked me to, but she didn't."

"Why not?"

"I think she was hurt, her best friend taking off that way. Besides, even if I wanted to find her, I wouldn't have known where to begin."

"You knew where to begin when you finally got started."

He couldn't be that stupid, I told myself. My ego wouldn't let me believe he thought I was, either. No wonder the private eyes in the movies always got sarcastic.

I restrained myself. "Lieutenant," I said sincerely, "I knew where to start because Faith *told* me where to start. You have infinitely more experience at investigations than I do. You must know—I mean, haven't you found that it's easier to check a story than to dig it up from scratch?"

Rogers showed me a handsome grin. "Okay, Ross," he said. "You don't seem to be hiding a guilty conscience about this stuff."

I decided it was okay to sigh. I hadn't realized how tense I was.

"But I still don't trust you."

Cutting a sigh off in the middle hurts.

"You want to know why? I'll tell you why."

Santa Claus is coming to town, I speculated silently.

Wrong again. "Because you're a reporter. I have no gripe with reporters, mind you." He shouldn't, I thought, with all the publicity he gets. "But I've never known a reporter who didn't think there was at least one little fact that would look better making its first appearance in the newspaper than in a police report."

"I just do the TV listings," I told him. I don't think I sniveled. I like to think of myself as a man who has never sniveled in his life. But I couldn't vouch for it.

Rogers's reaction left it open. "I know," he said. "That's why I'm letting you go."

I did not exactly spring from my wooden chair to my feet, but

I didn't dawdle, either. "Well," I said, "that wasn't as bad as I thought."

I was wondering whether the etiquette of the situation called for a handshake when Rogers went on. "I'm letting you go," he repeated, "because I don't think the fact you held back is going to wind up in the newspaper."

I sat back down.

"You told me you spoke to Lucille Letron the other night, right?"

Oh no, I thought. On the off-chance this was a stab in the dark to get me to blurt something out, I played it cool. "Sure. I told you what we said. You can check it with her, if you like."

Rogers picked up a piece of paper. "Oh," he said, "we have. Why didn't you tell me you went to bed with her?"

This told me two things. One, they were apparently hauling in the whole Letron family, millions or not, and doing it quickly, too. And two, that while I was being a gentleman, protecting a married lady's reputation, the lady in question had been shooting her mouth off to the cops.

I answered Rogers's question. "I didn't tell you because I was embarrassed."

He nodded. "I thought it might be something like that. Tell me, what would you think if I closed this case?"

I asked him what he meant.

"Closed it. Louis Letron was nuts, tried to kill his sister-in-law, blew himself up instead, case closed."

"I don't think I'd like it," I told him.

"Why not? You'd be off the hook."

"Faith might still be in danger. It's the old lady everybody seems to be afraid of. I can't really blame them."

"Yeah. I thought you'd say that, too. Get out of here, Ross."

I didn't wait for a second invitation. I decided to hell with the handshake, said good-bye, left the room and headed for the exit from the building.

And ran right into a blond, bearded individual who could be no one but Robert Letron.

"Mr. Ross?" he said. "I'd like to talk to you."

CHAPTER NINETEEN

The intelligent thing to do would have been to deny it, but I didn't think of that. Instead, I nodded miserably, and he confirmed all my fears about his identity.

The fears didn't have to do with anything physical. I doubted seriously he would start trying to punch me out inside a police station. Besides, I thought I could probably handle him if I had to, or at least hold my own. He was about the same height I was, a little broader in the shoulders, but I had a longer reach. Also, Lucille mentioned something about a heart condition. Angina. He didn't *look* like a man who had a heart condition, but angina, I understood, was painful, but not nearly as bad as a lot of heart conditions. In any case, it hadn't enfeebled him in any obvious way. But all that was secondary—he just plain didn't look like a violent man.

He didn't look like the active head of a huge commercial concern, either. He wore a down vest over a plaid shirt, corduroy trousers and high-topped, yellow-orange shoes. With his yellow beard and longish hair parted in the middle, he looked like a cross between a lumberjack and a Scandinavian Jesus. The ethereally pained look in his eyes only added to the impression.

My fears had to do with that look. I mean, the guy had every right to want to beat on me—the night before I had knowingly and willingly cuckolded him. What made it worse was that I hadn't felt any guilt about it until this very second.

So I stood there looking stupid while he gazed patiently into my eyes. "I really would like to talk to you, Mr. Ross," he said at last. In another mouth, that might have been a threat; here it was just a polite request.

Time to face the music, Harry.

"All right," I said. "I have to see about my sister first. Wait here for a minute. Or come with me." He had no reason to trust me, after all.

"I'll wait," he said. "See about Faith, too, will you? After all, she started all this."

I looked at him. Again, there was no malice in his voice or manner. On the contrary, he spoke with what sounded like genuine concern. The words were a little strange, considering Faith (and Sue and I) had come within an ace of being converted to chopped meat not three hours before, but I knew what he meant.

I went to negotiate with the cops. It wasn't difficult, but it took a while. It turned out that one of the precinct patrolmen going off duty about that time lived in White Plains, and would be taking the train home. They keep pushing for a residency requirement for New York City cops, but they won't get one passed until the day they pay a cop enough money to raise a family in New York City—i.e., never. So New York City cops live on Long Island, or in Westchester. This particular commuter would accompany Sue and Faith to my place to get a few things, then to Grand Central Terminal, then ride the train home with them, since Scarsdale is an earlier stop on the same line as White Plains. My mother (and a local police escort, if I knew my mother) would meet them there, then tuck them in safe and sound at her house, happy Thanksgiving to you. The house would be watched by Scarsdale cops, adjusting their patrols to take them by Mom's address at least once every half hour.

I would take a later train. I disdained police protection, or I would have, if anyone had thought to offer it to me. Not only was I brave, I didn't want any cops to overhear my conversation with Robert Letron.

He had a place all picked out—the Papaya King hot-dog stand on the corner of Eighty-seventh and Third. Not the busier one a block south and across the street, but the one where you could eat sitting down. We took a couple of stools at the counter. I read signs while I waited for the waitress to finish serving a take-out order. PAPAYA—GIFT OF THE ANGELS, said one. OUR HOT DOGS

—TASTIER THAN FILET MIGNON, claimed another. It occurred to me what a mess of a court case it would be if some cattle rancher or somebody tried to prove the hot dogs here were *less* tasty than filet mignon.

Leaving comparisons out of it, the hot dogs were pretty tasty, and I was reminded by the smell of them that I hadn't eaten anything since breakfast. The waitress asked us what we wanted. Robert ordered two hot dogs with sauerkraut and a fourteen-ounce pineapple juice. I took two plain and a fourteen-ounce papaya drink.

He smiled at me. "I love this place," he said.

Okay, I thought. He wants small talk, I'll give him small talk. "I wouldn't have thought you'd know this sort of place, moving in the kind of circles you do."

"I may be rich, Mr. Ross, but I'm still human." The waitress plunked the order down on the counter. I reached for my wallet, but Robert waved me off and paid. I felt more like a shit than ever. I screwed the guy's wife; now I was eating on his money.

I took a sip of the cold, smooth, pastel-orange papaya drink he'd bought for me and waited for him to say something. Instead, he unintentionally proved how human he was, first by not noticing a mustard-stained shred of sauerkraut that dangled from his mouth in the wake of a too-big bite of hot dog, then by starting to cry.

The waitress, the grillman, pretended not to look (this was New York, after all), but I was still embarrassed for him. I gathered up what was left of our lunch, and said, "Come on, let's hit the bricks."

"What?"

"Let's go outside. Nice, cool November day."

"What?" he said again. "Oh, sure. Sure." His voice was hoarse, and tears were beginning to wet the edges of his beard. He walked as if he had no knees.

Outside, he turned left, toward the avenue, but I took his arm and steered him east along Eighty-seventh street, toward the river. "We'll meet fewer people this way," I told him.

"I'm all right," he said. He sniffed, then repeated, "I'm all right."

He did sound better. I asked him if he had any particular place he'd like to go.

"No. Not right now."

"Okay then, we'll keep going this way. We'll take a look at the river. I live about a block and a half from the East River, but I never see it unless I make a special effort. I'm about due. Once a month, I like to go over to the river, lean on the railing, look across to Queens, and thank God I don't live there."

"What's wrong with Queens?"

I smiled at him. The man was not a New Yorker. "Got a few hours? Seriously, though, I think you'd better say what you were going to say to me."

His face fought against the anguish there to produce a smile. It was painful to watch, but I appreciated the effort.

"What I was *going* to say to you? All right. 'Stay away from my wife or I'll kill you.' "

"Message received," I told him. "And will be complied with. I suppose it's useless to apologize, so I won't. I'll just say I should have stayed away from your wife in the first place, and I know it."

"You don't have to apologize," he said.

"I don't?"

"No, I understand. I understand about you. Lucille can be irresistible when she wants to be."

"It wasn't all her," I said. "I was there, the door worked, and so did my legs. I could have gone. I stayed. I'm just as responsible as she is."

It occurred to me that this was the weirdest conversation I had ever been a part of. I mean, if I succeeded in convincing him of the extent of my responsibility, he could probably whip out a gun and shoot me and get away with it. Not that he would. We were being so civilized about the whole thing, we would have made Noel Coward look like a slob.

"I understand Lucille, too," he said with a civilized little smile. "But it doesn't make any difference, because I haven't said it. That's just what I was *going* to say to you. A simple, knee-jerk, jealous-husband response, but there's nothing simple about it. I simply have trouble thinking straight where Lucille is concerned. She probably told you I have trouble thinking straight under any circumstances. I certainly wasn't functioning too well back at the police station."

"You had a lot on your mind," I suggested. The Grayness would have approved of the understatement.

"A lot on my mind," Robert Letron echoed. "I guess you could say that. My brother dead, apparently in the act of attempted murder. Paul still in a coma, this whole mess with Faith. It's only natural that we'd feel a little fear, a little resentment for her. But to have let it go so *far*. We have enough money—we'll always have enough money. Louis certainly would have. His tastes may be—may have been—unusual, but they were well defined and provided for by his trust, by Paul's will. I never dreamed he would try to . . . try to—"

"Maybe it wasn't the money. Maybe it was the family tradition."

"Louis never cared about family tradition."

"Maybe he has the same kind of hang-up about artificial insemination your wife has."

He looked at me as if I had just told him I was crazy. "Louis never cared enough about anything to try to do something so drastic. He just wanted to relax and have fun. He used to kid me about it, my working so hard at the company, helping Paul, learning the business. He used to say if the work was that hard, I shouldn't do it. He said Peter had his glass sculpture, and he had his 'dusky beauties'; and Paul had the talent for making money. That's what he enjoyed, so we should let him do it, but that I should build myself a cabin in the woods, because being in the woods was what I'd like to do. He said some unfortunate people had to work to earn a living, but we didn't. I remember exactly what he said—'Idleness is not anything to be *proud* of, but it's nothing to be ashamed of, either. I just call it a gift from God in the person of my half brother, and try to enjoy it.' Does that sound like a killer?"

A lot of potential replies went through my head, ranging from "How the hell should I know" to "No, but maybe it sounds like an *unsuccessful* killer."

"Does it?" Robert demanded. His civility was starting to decline.

I cut him off before he could start crying again. "Peter saved our lives, you know. It was very brave of him."

"Yes," Robert said. He looked down at the sidewalk as though movies were being projected on it. "I should be proud of him. I will be proud of him, as soon as I get over my astonishment. Peter's always been in his own world, never been involved in anything but his hobbies. This has been a day . . . I mean, you think you know people . . ."

We came to First Avenue. I saw there wasn't much traffic (one of those inexplicable days, and the magic was holding) and started across. I turned to say something to Robert, but he wasn't there. He was back at the curb, waiting for the WALK light. WALK lights in New York exist strictly for lawyers to argue over in personal-injury cases. New Yorkers know if you pay attention to them, you don't get anywhere, because the cars are ignoring the traffic lights.

I went back and rejoined him at the curb. "You don't do much walking in New York, do you?"

"I don't do much of anything in New York, walking least of all. Not since I've been married, anyway. I don't care much for Paris, either. I'm not a city person. In Paris or New York, when I come into town for board meetings, the limousine meets me at the door, and takes me back home when I'm done. As far as I'm concerned, in the States, 'home' is our place in Connecticut. I'm perfectly happy to stay there, whether it's been made ready or not."

The WALK light came on. We crossed the street without incident.

"I wish I were there now," Robert said. "I was out chopping firewood—"

"When I first saw you, I thought you looked like a lumberjack."

He smiled and went on. "—chopping firewood when Harkins came running out of the house. A New York City policeman had telephoned him, said there was an emergency, and that I should come to the city right away. Harkins got the car and brought me to that police station. They questioned me, then they told me what had happened, then they questioned me some more.

"And it was funny. In the light of all those terrible things, my angina didn't act up, just a little twinge. You know I have angina?" He patted a pocket in the down vest as he asked the question.

"It's been mentioned."

"I didn't have to use any medicine. I felt completely calm, my mind was clear. I think I was numb. The only thing I was able to get worked up about was the fact that Lucille Berkowitz had collected another trophy."

"You know," I said stupidly.

"Of course I know. I've known all along. I may not be the business genius Paul is, but his father was my father, and I'm not stupid. I wouldn't marry a woman, no matter how much I loved her, if I didn't know something about her. All the more so since she so obviously didn't want to tell me anything. I checked, then I hired a detective to check more deeply."

"And you learned she was Jewish."

"She had been born Jewish. She didn't practice."

"For Jewish, that doesn't make any difference. And you married her anyway."

"I love her."

"Why didn't you tell her?"

"You think I'm a coward." He went on before I could deny it. "Maybe I am. If Lucille had told me, if she had been willing to defy Mother, I would have gone along with her. But Lucille herself was hiding her past, not just from me, from everyone, and I thought, why complicate things?"

He rubbed his face with the palm of his hand. "Now I know why. Lucille has built her life—our lives—around a deception, and no one can live that way. She punishes herself by bringing men to that apartment and seducing them. She feels like a cheat, so she acts like one."

I wasn't crazy about the idea that sex with me was a way women might choose to punish themselves, but I let it go.

"It really has become intolerable, Mr. Ross."

I told him to call me Harry, and he took it as if I had done him some great honor.

"Thank you," he said, and shook my hand. I could feel the calluses from the ax. "You must call me Robert. But the situation *is* intolerable, really. It affects everything. I can't help but think—"

I never did find out what he couldn't help but think. A police car, lights but no siren, pulled into the curb beside us so swiftly that Robert and I both jumped. A handsome young cop got out and stood in front of us on the sidewalk. He hadn't drawn his gun, but he was ready to.

He spoke to Robert. "Mr. Letron? Mr. Robert Letron?"

"Yes?"

"Are you all right?"

"Of course I'm all right. Why shouldn't I be all right?" Just then, Robert's eyes rolled up in his head, he clutched his chest, and collapsed heavily on the sidewalk.

A voice I knew came harsh and angry from the back of the squad car. "Don't be a fool! Ross *made* him say that! He's kidnapped my son, and now he's killing him!"

Robert groaned. He started scrabbling for his pocket.

The other cop got out of the car, spun me around and slammed me against it. "Grab the roof," he told me. The gun was out.

"He's kidnapped my son!" Alma Letron said again. "Shoot him!"

The cop didn't listen. I began to talk. "It's a heart attack. He's got a heart condition. I think he's got the medicine in the pocket he's reaching for."

The first cop, who was now tending to Robert, took a look. I tried to twist my neck so I could see what he was doing, but the second cop gave me a poke with the gun, and I changed my mind.

"Amyl nitrate," the cop said. "Poppers. He'd better have a prescription for this."

"He does, Officer," Robert's mother said. "Of course he does. Give it to him."

What do you know, I thought. For once the old woman and I are on the same side.

"If you don't treat my son immediately, I'll swear out a murder complaint against you!"

I don't think the threat is what made the cop go along, I think it was the fact that Robert was such a mess, he couldn't hurt him much even if he *did* give him an illegal drug. In any case, I heard a snap and a grunt, and by the time the second cop had finished frisking me, Robert was trying to get to his feet. The first cop practically had to sit on him to keep him down. They radioed for an ambulance for Robert. "You," they told me, "are coming with us."

They pushed me into the back of the blue-and-white. Alma Letron left to make room for me. She'd go to the hospital with her son. But she wasn't looking at her son. She was staring into the police car, at me. I stared back. It was hard to make her out through the close grillwork of the backseat cage I now occupied, but I could see her eyes. Her eyes were big and blue, and they shone with a cold, insane gleam of triumph.

CHAPTER TWENTY

I got into Scarsdale on the last train that night. Then my mother started.

"I called Hi Marks," she announced. She was telling me this before I even got to the car, a Mercedes diesel two-door. World War II is over at last for a lot of people from Our Set, at least when it comes to buying cars. I started to head for the passenger seat, but Mom took off her seat belt and slid across, leaving me the driver's side. Mom hates to drive; I don't mind, but I don't get a lot of practice. It *is* a nice car. I got in, leaned across, gave my mother a kiss on the cheek, buckled my seat belt, as the law of the People's Republic of New York now requires, and started the engine.

Hi Marks sounds like the kind of store my mother wouldn't go to, but he is instead an attorney, an old friend of my father's from the country club. Needless to say, the name was Hyman Markowitz when he first got it.

"So you called Hi Marks," I said. "That's nice, how is he?"

"How should he be? I didn't call him to find out how he is, I called him to get him to sue the New York City Police Department for you. Besides, he's fine. He's such a hypochondriac, he would have told me if he wasn't feeling fine."

"Sue them for what?"

"False arrest!"

"I wasn't arrested."

I couldn't see too clearly in the darkness, but I knew exactly the exasperated expression that had to be on her face.

"What do you call it, then, when you're about to come home for Thanksgiving, and you have to miss your train, because the police take you and haul you off to jail? An honor?"

I restrained myself from sighing. It drives her crazy when I sigh. "They didn't take me to jail, they took me back to the police station and asked me more questions. They had a right to."

"They had a right to listen to a crazy old woman—Faith's been telling me *stories* about that one—"

I had a cold flash of fear. "You didn't leave the girls alone," I said. I must have been an idiot not to have thought of it the minute I saw my mother there. Instinctively, I pressed a little heavier on the accelerator.

"Slow down, slow down," she said. "You think your mother is an idiot? They've got a policeman with them." I slowed down. Then, in a softer voice, she said, "Harry, do you think there's going to be any trouble?"

"No," I said truthfully. "I really don't. I just don't want to take any chances."

"I think that's smart."

"I hope you don't mind. Sue and I inflicting all this on you." It was less than gallant to bring Sue in, since I had been the one who'd inflicted it on *her*, but all's fair in love, war and dealing with your mother.

"How could I mind? Faith is like family. A sweet girl. She's had more than her share of tsouris." She thought for a moment. When my mother slips into Yiddish, things are getting serious. "Maybe we should sue the old lady, instead."

"I don't think we've got much of a case against her, either." The idea was tempting, though. There was no evidence Alma Letron had been behind anything but a bunch of neurotic children, but she still gave me the creeps. Maybe we could sue her, and if she got off by reason of insanity (if you can do that in a civil suit), then we would have some leverage to get her committed. It occurred to me that maybe I should have a chat with Hi Marks. Especially if I could do it without my mother finding out. She's one of the world's foremost gloaters.

"From what you told me on the phone, she gave her own son a heart attack."

"Whereas my mother only gives me ulcers."

"Very funny."

"Just a joke."

"I said, very funny."

"Anyway, she doesn't own up to that one. Last I heard, she was threatening to sue the police herself, for coming on too strong and startling poor Robert."

"Poor Robert," my mother echoed.

"That was the phrase she used. I've got a certain amount of sympathy for him myself. The thing is, Alma neglected to tell the cops in advance that Robert has a heart condition, so nobody could make any money on that lawsuit but the lawyers."

I was getting near home. The Ross ancestral estate, in the family for the one generation we'd been Rosses, was a ranch house in light green that had spread like an amoeba every time my father came down with an attack of do-it-yourself. I used to get in his way, and drop his tools, and color on his plans, a mode of behavior we both used to refer to as "Helping Daddy." The house was up ahead about a mile, and the closer I got to it, the more I wanted to retreat to childhood and forget about this whole mess.

"I'm tired, Mom," I said.

"I'm not surprised."

"Worn out with this stuff. Let's talk about something else."

"Something else? Sure. When are you going to get married, instead of running around with other men's wives? Did I raise you to do things like that?"

I started to laugh.

"Adultery is funny to you?"

I didn't tell her that while Lucille had committed adultery, all I'd been guilty of was fornication. I doubted Mom would appreciate the distinction. Instead, I said, "Mom, I apologize. You were right all the time. You used to tell me, do *one thing wrong*, get caught, and you're marked for life. I never believed you until now."

She addressed the roof of the car. "Why do they never believe you until it's too late?"

This started me laughing again.

"Now what?" my mother demanded.

"It's you," I said.

"Me."

"That's right. Breeding tells, as they say at The Grayness. You may jog. You may eat yogurt. You may be tanned from the sun in the summer and a lamp in the winter. You may be as chic as Bloomingdale's can make you. You may be tennis champ of the club for six straight years. You may be forever young and beautiful, even with white hair. You may still be able to get into your wedding dress."

"I weigh *less* now than I did when I got married."

"You may be the new format, but the essentials are all the same. You are still a *Jewish Mother*."

"And don't you ever forget it." The last word, as always. We were home. I pulled into the driveway, and we went in to meet the girls.

The best thing about the next two days was that nothing happened. Well, okay, things happened. We made turkey stuffing. We ate. We talked. We played Trivial Pursuit (Faith and I were big winners). On Thanksgiving, equality of the sexes was temporarily suspended, so I had to pretend I knew how to carve a turkey, and the three of them had to pretend they preferred it in shreds. As it was, I got the better of the deal, because I got to watch football while "the girls" (Mom's word, including herself) cleaned up. By tacit agreement, the name of Louis Letron, and the subject of bombs and murder, was not brought up.

There had been some minor excitement early Wednesday morning (I'm talking *early*, about 4 A.M.), when my mother woke me up demanding to know what we were going to do if Faith went into labor.

"Hah?" I said. I couldn't see her because the light had cauterized my eyelids together. Hitting the light switch without warning was Mom's favorite way of announcing her presence.

"I said, what are we going to do if Faith goes into labor? She's carrying awfully low, and she says she's about due, anyway. So what do we do if the baby decides to come today?"

"Panic?" I suggested.

"Very funny," Mom replied.

Then I told her it had all been taken care of. Sue had thought of it. Dr. Metzenbaum was spending Thanksgiving with her parents, too, and they happened to live in Harrison, less than a half hour away. If Faith got precipitate, we had the phone number, we'd all meet at St. Vincent's Hospital in White Plains, and everything would be hunky-dory.

"That's good," Mom said. "I was worried. Go back to sleep."

Not always the easiest instructions to follow, but I had no problem with them that time. I stayed awake only long enough to reflect that another answer to Mom's question would be "Rejoice." If Faith would just go ahead and have the baby, the threat would be removed whether or not it was Louis who'd been behind the whole mess. The money would pass and there would be nothing anyone could do about it. Sue had thought of everything else, why hadn't she asked the doctor about induced labor? I thought of mentioning it myself, but just before I drifted off, I decided not to. Faith would hate it, and I couldn't blame her. There was something unwholesome about messing with the birth of an innocent baby because of some sordid adult squabbling over money.

Friday afternoon, Faith wanted to go for a ride.

There was more football on, but it was college, and I could miss that. I was encouraged to see her taking an interest in things; back in New York, she had acted as if to leave the security of home was to tempt the gods and court sudden destruction. Just to make sure (the motive for more and more of my actions lately), I asked her why.

"I want to see the old town," she said. "I've been back here for three days, and for the first time since I got pregnant, I've been feeling safe. Mostly. And I can't get around by myself very well."

"We could all use some fresh air," Sue said.

"We'll go to Carvel," Mom put in. "You can get ice cream."

"I love ice cream in the winter," Faith said.

"I'll go to Carvel if Mom eats some, too."

"Oh, Harry, I've eaten too much already, the last two days."

"Harry's right, Mom," Sue said. "No fair being a skinny Jewish mother while you're trying to make your kids fat."

It was agreed. We got loaded into the car, then I said, "Just a second, I forgot the keys."

"They should be on the hook in the kitchen," Mom said helpfully.

I knew where they were, they were in my left front pocket. I wanted to go inside to use the phone. I was as tired as anyone of this shadow-fear game we'd been playing, but I wasn't going to ignore any of my moves until it was over. I spent one of my mother's message units, and arranged with the Scarsdale police for a discreet escort. Just to make sure.

I took them on Central Avenue toward White Plains. This is the classic Suburban Main Road, lined on either side for miles by franchise fast food joints and auto parts stores, stereo centers and shopping malls, small brick office buildings. Usually, wide as it is, traffic is impossible, but today it wasn't bad at all. Day after Thanksgiving, a lot of people didn't have to work.

Thinking of work reminded me that I had to be back in harness at The Grayness come Wednesday. I wasn't looking forward to it. I wasn't sure I approved of the notion of messily dead bodies being easier to take than orange-on-black computer displays of TV listings, but that's how I felt at the moment.

I was also thinking of the kind of crap I was going to get if they ever found out about my reticence to them about this whole affair. I'd told them enough to give them the jump on the other papers (that much loyalty I had), but I hadn't said anything about Faith, or her husband's whereabouts or condition, or why Louis Letron might possibly have wanted to kill her. More amazingly, it seemed the papers and TV stations hadn't been able to find out anything about it, either.

I found that hard to believe. *I'd* found out in a day or so, and I was hardly one of the great names in journalism. Maybe the police were sitting on them or something. I didn't really care. It may be hypocritical for someone who takes a paycheck from a contemporary American newspaper to be glad for a little privacy—no, I *know* it's hypocritical—but there it was. The respite was doing all of us good.

So did the ice cream. This particular Carvel franchise was in one of the shopping centers, across a large parking lot. Central Avenue may have been calm, but the shopping center was hopping, the movie theaters and the malls doing great holiday business. The ice-cream store was packed, and we had to wait quite a while before we were served.

Carvel has branched out into a line of trendy, scoop-it-out ice cream, the kind that comes in Yuppie flavors like Carob & Kiwi, but old-time fans ignore that stuff for the soft ice cream (vanilla or chocolate) that swirls out of a huge stainless-steel machine. It's so good, it almost lets you forgive their excruciating TV commercials. Anyway, we all got our cones (straight vanilla for me, vanilla Brown Bonnet for Sue, chocolate for Faith, and chocolate with sprinkles for Mom), and since there was no room in the store, went back to the car to eat them.

There was something pleasantly death-defying about trying to keep soft ice cream from dripping on the interior of a Mercedes-Benz. Fortunately, it was one of those steel-gray November days, dry, but cold enough to help keep the ice cream in place. "It would probably be a lot more fun to try this in August," I said.

"I'm having plenty of fun," Faith said. "I'd almost forgotten what it was like. Thank you, Mrs. Ross—"

"Don't be silly," Mom said.

"—and you too, Harry, Sue. I know I must have been impossible."

"Nah," I told her. "Just extremely difficult."

She laughed at that. A few days ago, she would have hit me.

"I feel so much better. For the first time since I knew I was pregnant, I feel as if I can have my baby in peace."

This was just wonderful. It was great for Faith's mental health and all, but it bothered me that I was now more worried by the situation than she was.

"It may not be over, you know," I said. I felt like a louse, but once you let a sense of responsibility wrap itself around your brain, you are more or less condemned to a life of lousehood.

"I know," Faith said. "There's always a chance it wasn't just Louis." I forewent pointing out that she was the one insisting on a conspiracy of the entire family against her. "But it isn't that. I've just decided not to be scared anymore."

Sue gave her a little hug, and my mother leaned back over the seat and kissed her on the cheek, and patted the baby. She told Faith how brave she was. I thought, what the hell, I was scared enough for everybody.

I finished my cone, told Mom to buckle up, and started the car. There was some commotion in the parking lot, a few people yelling and running, but the windows were rolled up to deaden the sound, and "the girls" were all busy talking, so no one seemed to notice but me, and I didn't care what it was, a contest, a purse snatching, or a personal appearance by Miss Nude America.

All I wanted to do was to get everybody safely back home. It occurred to me that a sense of responsibility would probably be a lot easier to carry off accompanied by some courage, but I couldn't seem to come up with any. It also occurred to me that I was learning a number of things about myself in recent days, and I didn't much like any of them.

I wondered what Lucille was doing this minute. I remembered her grinding against me in the dusty apartment. I had to shake my head violently to get rid of the image. Mom asked me if anything was wrong.

"No, Mom," I said. "Sudden chill."

I was thoroughly disgusted with myself by the time I left the parking lot.

CHAPTER TWENTY-ONE

I got even more disgusted with myself later, for letting myself get talked into not going straight home. Faith still wanted to be driven around. She wanted to see Scarsdale High School so badly you might have thought it was America's answer to the Arc de Triomphe, built specifically for people to go admire the architecture, and be moved by what it symbolized. The whole thing would have been easier to take if I hadn't known Faith had spent three years sitting in that building, complaining about it daily in chorus with my sister.

I said words to that effect. My mother told me to stop grumbling. We went to the high school; we looked at it from all accessible vantage points. Faith seemed to be getting her money's worth. Finally, she seemed satisfied, and we got back in the car.

I was still the only one who wanted to go home.

I asked Faith where she wanted to go. She didn't mind, anywhere. It was just so nice to be home again. She'd been so far from this, had actually tried to forget it, and that hadn't been fair, to her father's memory, or to herself. Mom and Sue took that big. I was afraid I was going to have to open the glove compartment and hand out Kleenex.

At this point, I ceased worrying about the whole business. What the hell, I thought. Her life, her baby. Besides, in the rearview mirror, I could just make out our friendly police escort, sitting discreetly by the side of the road, waiting patiently for us to move on. It would have made a big hit with the local taxpayers (of whom my mother was one) if they'd known we were tying up an entire squad car to escort us on an aimless little sentimental journey through the highways and byways of

Westchester County, but it would have been self-defeating to bring the matter up.

The sooner I got moving, the sooner I could get them home. I decided to stick to the byways rather than the highways. Westchester has a lot of these, old WPA projects that had been engineering marvels in their day, but had since been made largely obsolete by higher speeds, and the big state and inter-state roads. Faith would see more of the county this way, and the relative lack of traffic would let the cop behind us get a good look at anybody who happened to join us.

Nobody did. We tooled along an old tree-lined road, gray-white, with sloppy stripes of tar smoothing the way between the concrete slabs. Faith read road signs like old poetry. The police car stayed behind at the edge of visibility. I decided again to quit worrying—if someone had been following us when we'd left the house, he would have had to stop when we'd gotten ice cream, he would have had to follow us around the high school. The cop would have spotted him by then.

That was when the police car started pulling up on us. I had a flash of panic—he's spotted something. I checked all the mirrors, I took my eyes off the road and looked around, drawing a dirty look from my mother, and saw nothing. The gap between us narrowed.

My next guess was that he was going to pull me over, tell me the whole thing was ridiculous, that he was going back to head-quarters and real police work, and that I should go home if I was so nervous. That would have been embarrassing, but I could handle it. The police car kept getting closer.

I started looking at the figure behind the wheel, expecting a hand signal to get me over to the side of the road. Lights and siren would have been a bit much. I remember a flicker of surprise crossing my brain as I saw his face. I'd caught a glimpse of the man behind the wheel of the police car as we pulled away from the house, hadn't remembered him being black.

The surprise was replaced by fear as the police car came closer yet. This guy wasn't black, or not necessarily. He was wearing a ski mask.

"Cops don't wear ski masks," I said aloud.

"What are you talking about, Harry?" Sue wanted to know.

"Holy shit!" I said, and stepped down hard on the accelerator.

"What is going on? You're scaring Faith!"

There was no reason for her not to be scared. That was not a policeman. I remembered the commotion just as we were leaving the shopping center. That might have had something to do with this . . .

My speculations were cut short when the police car rammed our rear bumper. The impact was hard enough to jar my head back, but not hard enough to make me lose control of the car. He backed off a little, and repeated the trick.

Mercedes makes a fine car, but diesel engines stink when it comes to acceleration, and I would've traded all the luxury in the world for some decent acceleration at this moment.

The next bump was a little harder. I was sure the bastard was grinning under the ski mask.

I undoubtedly would have panicked, but between Faith and my mother, the panic allotment of that car was used up. They were screaming, in counterpoint and two-part harmony, "He's trying to kill me, he's trying to kill *my baby!*" and, "Harry do something, for God's sake *do something!*" Sue was sitting quietly in the back seat, wearing the expression of someone who had already *been* in an auto accident.

Going apeshit, blaming somebody else, and lapsing into catatonia were my three first choices, too, but since they were taken, the only thing left for me was to think of something.

And I did, too. I didn't exactly think of it, I *remembered* it. It was a sovereign remedy for tailgaters. My father had told me about it, though I don't actually remember him ever actually doing it. Too dangerous.

Right now, though, I would have used a nuke if I could figure out how to get one. Danger to my tormentor wasn't a consideration.

We were going at a pretty good clip by now, about ninety, double the speed suited to this road. It would be difficult to keep the car on the road driving this fast, even without some maniac trying to (literally) bump me off.

It was too late to avoid the next bump, and the renewed round of screams that went with it. I kept my foot to the floor and waited for the next one.

Timing was going to be important. I had to take one hand off the wheel to get ready, which didn't make things any easier. I waited. The police car dropped back about twenty yards, then increased his speed again, and came forward for another bump.

I switched on my headlights.

Which also turned on my taillights. Taillights, appearing suddenly in the daytime, look just like brake lights. He had no choice but to think I'd slammed on my brakes, a move that had a good chance of killing all of us, but was practically guaranteed to send him into a vicious head-to-tail collision that would crush him and the car around him into something approximating a can of Spam.

I could hear the squeal as the driver of the police car stood on his brakes and locked the wheels. I saw him start to go into a spin, but the road curved, and I lost sight of him.

I didn't go back to look. If he had a cop's car, he might have a cop's gun. I drove straight to my mother's house, and phoned the real police, and told them all about it.

CHAPTER TWENTY-TWO

Lieutenant Craig Rogers came up to Scarsdale to talk to us, instead of ordering us to haul ass into the city. Didn't want to ruin our weekend, he said. Imagine what he could have done if he *had* wanted to.

Rogers was the guest of honor at a surprise Saturday-after-Thanksgiving party, thrown by my mother. That she was throwing it was the big surprise. Guests were primarily law-enforcement officials, Rogers and two New York friends, and contingents from the Scarsdale P.D. and the New York State Police, many of whom we'd met yesterday, in the immediate wake of our daring escape from the killer police car.

I could see why they might want more than one session of questioning. Yesterday I'd learned that the officer assigned to follow us was one Frank Osgood, a young man, five years on the force, good record, maybe not brilliant, but brave and honest, and well-liked by all his comrades, and the rest of that whole catalog of folk-song virtues.

Officer Osgood was now in intensive care at St. Vincent's with a fractured skull. He was going to live, and it didn't look as if there would be any serious brain damage, but the cops made sure to impress upon all of us that even under the best of circumstances, a fractured skull was an unpleasant experience. Some of the uniformed cops gave me the impression that they would be delighted to help me put their assertion to the proof, if I held any doubt, but I was content to take their word for it.

As far as anyone could tell, someone had been watching the house yesterday in addition to Officer Osgood, someone who had been clever enough to spot the increased police patrols. And, when we finally decided to go out, he'd been smart

enough not to follow us, where the police officer would surely
have spotted him, but to follow the cop himself.

He was also smart enough to come up with what The Grayness would undoubtedly call "a bold plan" during the time we
were parked at the shopping center buying ice cream. What he
did was to go to a distant part of the parking lot, being careful to
remain in plain view of the parked squad car. Then he took out
a wrench, and started smashing windshields.

It was plainly Officer Osgood's duty to stop him. (I keep saying him. Since all my companions saw was a ski mask, and what
Officer Osgood saw was locked in a cracked head until he
regained consciousness, it could well have been a woman.)

Osgood's Duty. The surveillance had been explained to Osgood by the desk sergeant (and, I admit, to the desk sergeant by
me) as no big deal, whereas daylight vandalism, by an obvious
maniac wielding something that might at any second be used as
a deadly weapon, obviously *was* a big deal. So he went to stop
him. He should have called for help, but he didn't. The Chief
yesterday remarked that perhaps Osgood was a little too brave.

And somehow, the vandal got behind him and patted him on
the head with the wrench. It probably wasn't all that difficult,
crouched down behind the maze of parked cars. He left Osgood
lying there, took the keys, and calmly took possession of the
police car. The commotion I'd noticed as we left the shopping
center had been patrons getting out of the movie matinee and
discovering what had happened to their cars. Nobody discovered Officer Osgood until more cops came in response to the
calls of irate car owners.

I eventually came to realize that the State Police were at my
mother's house today primarily to help Rogers keep the locals,
led by Chief Michael Green, who was a friend of my father's for
twenty-five years and should have known better, from getting
out of line and violating the rights of possibly innocent citizens,
and worse yet, blowing the case if they turned out not to be
innocent.

I eventually came to realize that, and even to be glad the hat
tree was filled with Smokey the Bear hats. It hadn't occurred to

me by the time I told my mother to call Hi Marks and get him over here. The cops had knocked on the door, and asked if they could come in, very politely, too. My mother sets a lot of store in politeness, and as far as she knew she had no reason to keep them out.

Once they got inside, it was a different story. They wanted to set up in different rooms, question the four of us separately. One of them started poking around in drawers and under cushions.

I could understand their problem. All they'd known before yesterday was that they were supposed to keep an eye on the house, and provide reasonable protection when asked. Today, one of them was in the hospital (and one of their squad cars was wrecked). They faced the knowledge that the amount of embarrassment they would experience would be directly proportional to the amount of the story that got out. They would have talked with Rogers by now, and learned that this supposed routine surveillance was part of a much bigger mess than they'd imagined.

Knowing more, they'd be thinking more to the point, and something would have occurred to the Chief that had kept me awake all last night. Today, he would get answers, or know the reason why.

Understanding the problem wouldn't make the experience any more pleasant, especially for my mother. Or for Faith. I wanted a lawyer around.

It did not solve all the problems. It is impossible for policemen to believe that an innocent person needs a lawyer. My mother's picking up the phone disappointed the Chief, if it didn't shock him.

Chief Green looks more like a math teacher at some small New England college than a policeman. He wears a uniform only on special occasions. Today, apparently, was more special for us than it was for him, since he wore his usual gray business suit. He's slender, wears glasses, and combs his hair straight back from a receding hairline.

"You didn't have to do that, Helen," he said when my mother hung up the phone.

My mother was so mad her lips had disappeared. Growing up, I hadn't seen that look much (what can I say? I was just naturally a good boy), but when I did see it, I used to go hide under the bed.

"Don't come busting into my house and try to call me Helen," my mother told him. "What are we, criminals, that ten of you" —she looked around and counted—"*twelve* of you have to come with guns to talk to us?"

"Fourteen, Mom," Sue said. "Two went upstairs." She was madder than my mother was, and made me more nervous. Sue was perfectly capable of going over and smacking somebody, and getting us all arrested, or maybe shot.

"And searching the place without a warrant. There's a pregnant girl up there asleep. If anybody bothers her, I'll call the newspapers. My son here works for The Greatest Newspaper in the World." She interrupted her anger to give me a look of warm pride.

Hi Marks only lived a few blocks away, so Mom had no trouble filling the time until he got there. It was better, I suppose, than everything standing mute and letting the cops yell at us. Chief Green, and the guy in charge of the State Police contingent, whose name I never did get, were delighted to let her go on with it, working on the time-tested fact that people will frequently let go of things during a tirade that they would hold on to for dear life during more reasoned discourse.

I didn't mind, since anyone as experienced with tirades as a Jewish Mother, even the new type, is not going to say anything they don't want to say. Besides, we had absolutely nothing to hide. My mother could blurt until the Ayatollah made his bar mitzvah, and she couldn't tell the cops anything they didn't know, except that they should be ashamed of themselves, harassing a family that had taken in a poor, persecuted girl with no one to turn to, and so on.

I sneaked a look at Lieutenant Rogers during all of this. He seemed amused. He stood there (behind my mother, and therefore out of the line of fire) until Hi Marks showed up.

Hi Marks smiled and shook hands with everyone. He has the

best tan of anyone in Scarsdale, except possibly my mother. He smokes a cigar, and moves very slowly, with his chest puffed out, like a pigeon looking for a mate. He has wavy silver hair on his head, which I happen to know is a toupee, but which would fool anyone else in the world. He talks and dresses formally. I've never heard him use a contraction or seen him without a suit and tie.

"Michael," he said. "Helen." He spread his hands like a patriarch. "What can the matter be between two old friends, that a third friend has to mediate?"

My mother was about to tell him what the matter could be, when Hi showed he wasn't there to mediate. "Now, Helen, let us not rush things. Michael, please tell me what is wrong, and then my client and I will confer."

"This isn't necessary, Hi," the Chief said.

"Better to err on the side of caution."

Craig Rogers came up and murmured in my ear. "I think your mother's in good hands now."

I told him I was sure she was. Hi Marks is still a bachelor because he has been in love with my mother since way before my father died. He was too good a friend to do anything about it then. I didn't know what was holding him back now. Maybe he was afraid of being rejected. I had this vision of myself as a well-off, well-liked, white-haired bachelor in my sixties, never using contractions and wearing two fresh carnations a day in my lapel. It beat being a drunk in a gutter, I supposed, but I still didn't like it.

"Think we can have a little talk in private?"

"Without my lawyer?"

"Only guilty people need lawyers," he told me, but he was smiling as he said it. "Strictly off the record. Come on, Ross. If I double-cross you, write an exposé or something."

I took him up to my old room. I sat on the bed. Rogers got to sit on the hideously uncomfortable wooden chair that had come with the desk and the rest of the bedroom set. Part of my success as a journalist (ha) comes from my speed at typing, which in turn is the result of my wanting to get my reports over

with so I could get the hell out of that chair before my spine
warped. I hoped Rogers would feel the same way about it.

It didn't seem to be bothering him. He spent a little time
looking at the model Spad hanging from the ceiling, read the
autographs on the baseball from the 1967 Yankees, one of the
most mediocre baseball teams ever to lace on spikes.

"Dooley Womack, for God's sake," he said. "I'd forgotten all
about him."

"Shame on you," I told him. "Is this what you wanted to talk
about?"

"No. Unfortunately. You ever read comic strips?"

"Of course."

"I know a guy who does a comic strip. He's married to a cop,
can you believe that?" He shook his head in amazement. "Anyway, this guy can talk about funny stuff. Hours and hours. Jokes
and stories. All day."

"He must be fun at parties."

"I don't know. The thing is, he can talk about funny stuff
because it's his job and he's good at it. My job is not-funny stuff."

"Like murder."

"I am with the homicide squad," he said, as though I'd been
debating it.

"So talk," I said. I had the feeling I wasn't going to like it.

"We're going to take Mrs. Letron into custody," he said.

"Lucille?" I sounded like Little Richard. "She was trying to
run me off the road yesterday? She bashed the cop?"

"I don't know," Rogers said. He was looking into the bottom
of my old Magic 8-ball as if he expected to find the answer there.
It was probably telling him "it is too early to say," which was the
best I ever seemed to do.

"I don't know anything, except nobody has an alibi. Family all
lives together, and for hours, nobody sees anybody. We found
the police car about a block and a half from the train station, you
know."

"So it's possible one of them did it and scooted right back to
the city."

Rogers nodded. "Even Lucille's husband. He was let out of

the hospital in time for Thanksgiving, but he's been staying at the Westbrook with his family."

"The car chase would have been a little rough on his heart."

"Maybe. Anyway, there's no way we're ever gonna prove any of this."

My mind decided to get back to the point, and instructed my mouth to take steps in that direction. "Not Lucille," I said. "You're arresting the old lady? Alma?"

"Are you being deliberately dense? Why would I tell you in advance if I was arresting the old woman?" He shook his head, disappointed in me. "Besides, I didn't say arrested, I said taking into custody."

"What's the difference?" I asked. Then before he could tell me, I said, "Anyway, who's left? The only other Mrs. Letron I know is—"

"Exactly," he said.

"Faith?" I said. "You're taking Faith Letron into custody?"

"Ex*act*ly," he said. There was a big smile on his face. The star pupil had come through at last.

CHAPTER TWENTY-THREE

That pretty well polished off what was left of the holiday spirit; Sunday morning I took the train back to the city.

I followed my usual Sunday morning routine—the Food Emporium, where I fought the crowd for bagels, then to the discount store to fight another mob for the *Times*, the *News*, and The Grayness. I hadn't checked to see if our Road Warrior adventure had made the city papers while I was back home—if it had, it was gone by now. I looked carefully through all three Westchester sections while I toasted bagels (in an appliance I keep just for that purpose), smeared them with cream cheese, and crammed them in my mouth, washing them down with swigs of orange juice. I put the papers aside for closer perusal later, then parked in front of the TV to watch football. Antarctic explorers aren't as cut off from the mundane affairs of the world as thoroughly as I am when I'm watching a football game, and cut off from the mundane affairs of the world was exactly what I wanted to be that day.

I was well into the game when the phone rang. I cursed resignedly, and went over to pick it up.

"Harry Ross?" a woman's voice demanded.

It wasn't my mother, my sister, or Faith, so I figured it must be one of those advertising things, like "Have The Grayness home-delivered for twenty cents a week" or something like that. I wanted to start speaking Spanish or something, but the woman probably did, too. I thought of lying about it. My mother's influence won—I told the truth from force of habit.

"This is Harry Ross," I said. The Giants had the ball third and six on the Browns' thirty-seven yard line. Simms went back to pass.

"Where is my patient, Mr. Ross?"

The receiver caught the ball out of bounds. I suppressed a groan. Instead, I said, "Dr. Metzenbaum?" I may have been cut off from the mundane affairs of the world, but there was only one doctor in the world who would call me up that day to ask me where her patient was.

"I don't know where Faith is," I told her.

"I don't like being lied to, Mr. Ross," the doctor said. "You must know where she is. The police didn't tell me much, but Lieutenant Rogers told me that he got your approval before he took Faith into custody. Into *custody!* The woman is going to have a baby, she's been the victim of these attacks—"

"Did they remember to tell you it was protective custody?"

She snorted. It was ladylike, but it was still a snort. "Whatever *that* means," she said. "I'm her doctor, for God's sake. I'm supposed to have access to my patient."

"Rogers told me you would be notified the second—all *right!*" Landeta had just put a punt out of bounds about three centimeters from the Cleveland goal line.

"What was *that?*" Dr. Metzenbaum wanted to know.

"Nothing, sorry. Just something that happened in the football game."

"Oh, God. No wonder. Look, I really want to talk to you about this. When will the game be over?"

"It's all right," I said. "I want to talk about it, too." Then I made a little grunt as a Cleveland ballcarrier nearly fumbled.

"No," she said, "if you're anything like the men I've known, you're going to be worthless until the game is over."

She wouldn't even let me try to deny it, which was just as well. If there has *ever* been something I wanted to forget for the length of time it takes to watch an NFL game or two, this mess with Faith was it. There was no *handle* to it.

"I think it's probably better to discuss this in person, anyway," she said. "Can you be at my office at eight o'clock?"

"Any time you say," I told her. This time I really meant it. If there was anything that would help get my mind off football, it was a chance at a tête-à-tête with a woman I'd been fantasizing about for several days.

"Eight o'clock will do it," she said. She sounded as if she was smiling. "I have to drive in from New Jersey."

"What are you doing in New Jersey?" I asked.

"I live here," she said. "In Fort Lee."

"Oh," I said. To Manhattanites, New Jersey is more incomprehensible than Queens, or would be, except for the fact that the Giants play there.

"Eight o'clock, then," I said.

I got there at twenty of, having given up on the doubleheader game early and taken a cab downtown. She smiled as she let me in. "Dull game?" she asked.

"Couldn't concentrate on it," I said. She led me to the room where we'd spoken before. "Well," I said. "I know why I want to talk to you, why do you want to talk to me?"

"I want to talk to you because there must be some way you can help me find out where Faith is. I don't anticipate any problems, but she could go into labor any minute." I opened my mouth, but she went on. "I know Rogers has promised to notify me immediately if Faith goes into labor, but I don't like it. I'm going to call you Harry."

"Thank you," I said. "Barbara. I don't like it, either. But what do you expect me to do about it, for crying out loud?"

"*I* don't know. If you're not her fiancé, you're at least her boyfriend—"

"Damn right I'm not her fiancé. The lady's husband happens to be alive. And I guess you weren't listening too hard the first time we talked. Faith is my sister's friend. Period. She is not my girlfriend. Nobody is my girlfriend. Nobody has been my girlfriend, or performed the functions of one, for months now." It was out of my mouth before I remembered Lucille. Talk about a mental block. "Almost nobody," I amended. It kind of spoiled the effect, but apparently, Barbara decided to take it at face value.

"Oh," she said. "What are we going to do, then?" She played with her pearls. She dressed like a farmhand during office hours;

on Sunday she looked as if she'd just hit Lord & Taylor with a clean credit card. I didn't try to figure it out.

"What can we do? Call Rogers tomorrow and try to talk him out of it."

"Well, then," she said brightly. "This was a fairly stupid trip we've taken. I'm sorry to have taken you away from the game."

She started to get up. I reminded her that I wanted to talk to her about a few things, and she sat back down.

"First of all," I said, "I want to explain the mixup about Faith's going into custody. Rogers didn't need my permission, he needed my cooperation. My mother would never have let Faith out of her sight if Rogers hadn't scared me to death, then eased up. I was so relieved he wasn't arresting her, I was glad to talk her into going with him. I'm sorry he used it to smooth things over with you, but I'm not sorry professionals are looking after Faith now."

"Can't they look out for her without *hiding* her, for heaven's sake?"

"Probably," I conceded, "but Rogers told me something—he swore it was true—that convinced me to go along."

"What was that?"

"You know those attacks on Faith? The ones that led her to come looking for me in the first place?"

"Of course."

"Louis Letron has alibis for two of the three."

"Oh," she said. It was about what I'd said when Rogers had told me. And she was a lot quicker than I had been at working out the implications. Let us say that the attack on the car full of us was unrelated to the attacks on Faith. Nobody believed it, but let's say it, especially since the cops *would* say it if the investigation went nowhere, and they had to pin the whole business on Louis or get stuck with a messy, not to say ridiculous, unsolved case. That is, they would say it if a woman named Clothilde Fernandes of Rio de Janeiro, Brazil, had not told investigators that she and Louis Letron had attended the ballet the night the car tried to run Faith down, and she'd come to me. Especially since she went on to say they were accompanied by another

couple, and the couple had backed her up. They had gone
dancing later, still in each other's company. This was an alibi to
put in textbooks. It didn't prove Louis had had nothing *whatever* to do with his own death (you know what I'm trying to say,
here), but it sure made it look as though he had help.

Unknown help. Help that was still at large. Help that just
might be trying with all its might to find out where Faith was
and finish the job.

"Ah," Barbara said. "I guess we'll leave the lieutenant alone
tomorrow. Do you want to know why I live in New Jersey? I was
going into practice with a guy I was living with. We met in med
school. We bought a condo and an office building. Couldn't have
done that in Manhattan.

"We split up. He got the office, I got the condo. Happy? I
could tell in your voice over the phone you wanted to know.
What puzzles me is why I told you."

"Got me," I said. "Do you have a date or something?" I
indicated her clothes.

"No, I like to dress this way, but after somebody's water
breaks on a two-hundred-dollar wool skirt, you learn to save
them for weekends."

"Do you have to go back to Fort Lee? Have you eaten yet?"

"No," she said, "to both questions."

"I usually go all ethnic on Sundays and get a delivery from a
kosher deli in my neighborhood. They have tables, though.
Would you like to join me?"

She smiled at me. "I thought you'd never ask."

CHAPTER TWENTY-FOUR

So we got into Barbara's little Renault Alliance and went uptown to the Cornucopia Deli, where we let Puerto Rican waiters serve us Jewish soul food. I had corned beef on rye with mustard, she had brisket with horseradish on a hard roll, we both had chicken soup with matzoh balls, and we would undoubtedly both have heartburn later, but I had Di-Gel at home, and she was a doctor. She ought to be able to look out for herself.

It came out over dinner that she was a recently converted "Doctor Who" fan. She'd stumbled upon the show on one of the local public television stations, where she'd turned in search of a documentary on natural childbirth. Scoping out the competition. Anyway, she saw the show, got hooked, and started tuning in every Saturday night. It further turned out that the only actor she'd ever seen playing the Doctor was Tom Baker.

This, of course, was all too good to be true. If she'd said she also read comic books, I would have proposed marriage to her on the spot. As it was, I proposed something else. I told her I had "The Five Doctors" on tape, the adventure that reunited all of the Doctor's various personae, and if she wasn't doing anything, I would be delighted to show it to her.

She said yes.

I was feeling pretty good as we walked the ten blocks or so to my apartment (it's better to walk ten blocks in Manhattan than to give up a parking space). The good feeling continued all the way back to my building. Then two men got out of a parked car and confronted us.

Yorkville is a pretty safe neighborhood as New York neighborhoods go, but the buses and the subways run everywhere, to say nothing of bridges and roads, and there's no place the bad guys don't have access to. Suddenly, New Jersey was looking pretty good.

I was closing fists and shaping my mouth to tell Barbara to run when one of the apparitions said, "Mr. Ross? Peter Letron. I was here the other day."

Now that, I thought, was modesty. I was not likely at this point to forget any of the Letrons, especially the one who'd kept me from walking into a bomb blast.

"The doorman wouldn't let us wait inside," his companion said. "I don't really blame him." This was Robert Letron. I remembered him, too.

"You people are going to get me evicted," I said. Now that I was breathing again, and relaxed enough to take in details, I could see Robert smile.

"I am sorry about that," he said. "Our big mistake, I think, was telling the doorman our names."

I nodded. The last time a Letron hung around that lobby, the landlord had to pay for redecoration. He was trying to come down on me for the money. Hi Marks was standing by.

Barbara cleared her throat, reminding me of my manners. I introduced her, or rather I introduced them to her. If you're going to remember your manners, you might as well go all the way and remember them right. Barbara was pleased, she said, to meet them, and I suspect she was, only not in the way they might have preferred. Dr. Metzenbaum, it seemed, had the same sort of upper-middle-class reaction to the Really Rich that I had. It was more the reaction of someone who was, against all rational expectation, actually laying eyes on a unicorn or a hippogriff, than the pleasure of making the acquaintance of some fellow human beings.

Peter was oblivious to it. He was oblivious to everything tonight, manners included. "Mr. Ross," he said, "we have to talk to you." He looked at Barbara. "Alone would be best."

"About Faith Letron?" Barbara demanded. I had already noticed that however she dressed, the most appropriate professional attire for Dr. Metzenbaum would be a tiger suit.

Robert looked at his brother, a mixture of surprise and scorn at the idea that the usually self-effacing Peter would pick this time to be so rudely outgoing. It seemed as if he almost had to tear his eyes away from the boy.

Peter was oblivious to that, too. "Yes," he said, "it is. I mean, Mr. Ross is a nice person and all, but we don't have much to talk to him about except Faith, do we?"

"If it's about Faith, I stay," Barbara declared.

Peter was going to protest, but I got in first. "Dr. Metzenbaum is Faith's healer," I said. Nobody laughed.

I tried again. "She's Faith's obstetrician. Anything that has to do with Faith concerns her."

Peter subsided. He looked at Barbara with interest, then made a gracious apology, which made me very happy, since I didn't think I would enjoy being in the middle of a controversy between a man who had saved my life and the woman I was rapidly falling in love with.

"Let's go up to my apartment and talk," I suggested. The doorman gave me a dirty look as I ushered them inside. I was glad it wasn't the guy who'd been on duty when the bomb went off.

Just before we got on the elevator, I muttered, "So much for 'The Five Doctors.'" Robert begged my pardon. Barbara smiled and told him it was nothing, just a medical matter, and I almost kissed her on the spot.

I used the elevator ride to thank Peter for saving my life. And Faith's and Sue's, of course.

Peter seemed embarrassed. "It was the least I could do." I assured him it had been plenty.

Robert said, "Where's your package?"

"I left it in the car," Peter told him.

"Why? You want Ross to have it, don't you?"

"Have what?" I asked.

Peter turned to me. His eyes were apologetic. The offensive young man had been left behind on the sidewalk. "Some of my work. Glass animals. I don't know, a lion, a couple of bears."

"I like bears," I told him.

"Well, I still want to give you the stuff. I just didn't think it would be such a good idea to bring a package addressed to you in here, especially since we'd have to tell our names to the doorman."

Robert said, "Ah," and stroked his beard.

"Don't worry about it," I said. "When we're done, I'll come downstairs with you and pick it up."

"Thank you," Peter said. "It's not much, but we want to show you we're sorry for all the trouble we caused. I mean, I made the animals, but they're really from Robert and me, and Lucille and . . ."

"And Mother?"

"Mother always wants us to do the right thing," Peter said staunchly.

Robert had a pained look on his face. I wondered if it was over Mother's lack of enthusiasm for kissing and making up. Or, I thought, it might be that Lucille was a little too enthusiastic. I had a feeling the Lucille episode was going to make me feel stupider and stupider every time I thought of it for the rest of my life. I hoped that wasn't what was bothering him now. Then I thought about it a second, and hoped it was. The last time I'd seen that look on his face was just before the heart attack. I was glad to get him into my apartment and into a chair.

Peter looked around my apartment as if he was going to make me a cash offer for the place and contents. He went to my window and took a long look at my fabulous view of the north side of East Seventy-ninth Street. Then he took a chair across from his brother. That left the sofa for Barbara and me, which I didn't mind a bit.

Before I sat, I asked them if they wanted anything to drink, and got two noes. I sat down and looked at them look at each other. Robert looked more pained than ever, and Peter looked as if whatever his brother had was catching. When I couldn't stand it anymore, I said, "You wanted to talk?"

"Yes," Peter said. "Yes," Robert echoed.

More silence. "Well," I said at last. "Did you watch the Giants today? Some game, huh?"

"We didn't see it," Robert said. "We were busy." He took a breath. "Mr. Ross—"

"I thought I was going to be Harry," I said. I shouldn't have interrupted him two words after he'd gotten started. Now he had to apologize for not calling me Harry, and remind me I had to call him Robert, and Peter and I had to get on a first name basis as well. Barbara stayed out of it. Apparently she was content to remain Dr. Metzenbaum to these two.

Robert started again. "Harry, have you heard anything from my mother lately?"

"Since when?"

"Since—ahh—since I was taken to the hospital."

Since your brother blew himself up, I reminded him silently.

"No," I said. "Not a word. Why?"

Peter said, "Thank God for small favors."

"This is very difficult," Robert said. It was getting pretty difficult for me, too. "I hope," he went on. "I hope Peter is right when he says Mother wants us always to do the right thing."

"Of course she does, Robert," his brother says. "She'd say so if she weren't . . ."

"There we come to it, Harry. My mother *is* disturbed, or mad, or crazy, or whatever word you care to fill in for the one Peter couldn't bring himself to say."

With a heroic effort, I restrained myself from saying the words that presented themselves to my mind, namely, "About goddam *time.*"

Robert must have read the words on my face. "That woman you've met isn't my mother," he told me. "She's been vanishing little by little since we found out Paul was sick."

"The strange thing is," Peter said, "she doesn't even *love* Paul. He's not her son, after all. I guess she's always thought of him as a meal ticket for us when she's gone. She never dreamed he'd be likely to go first, and leave most of the money elsewhere. Not much of a vote of confidence for us, either, I guess."

"But that's all beside the point," Robert said. "There is nothing left of my mother but resentment and fear and anger. I won't deny they have always been a part of her. They're a part of everyone. But there used to be so much more: humor, and style, and enjoyment of life." His voice trailed off, then came back like a new station on the radio.

"But that's all beside the point, too. The important thing now is to do what's right. Mother has come up with the worst of her fantasies yet—"

"She says Faith killed Louis!" Peter said.

"How?" I demanded. "She almost walked into that explosion herself."

"Logic is another part of Mother that has been lost," Robert said. "The worst part of the whole business is that she's swearing revenge."

"We're going to have her put away before she does anything," Peter explained. "It's the right thing to do."

"But it's going to take time," Robert said. "She can be very plausible when she wants to be. And we'd like to do it with as little publicity as possible. We owe her that much."

"I'm certainly not going to try to talk you out of it," I said. "I'm just wondering what you came to me for. Do you want me to testify at a hearing or something?"

"No, no, nothing like that." Robert was horrified by the idea. "God forbid that it come to a hearing. We'll keep you informed of what happens, and how long it's likely to take."

"Okay, sure, but you still haven't told me why you need me for any of this."

"Well, we'll try to keep an eye on her, but she might still get some kind of nasty message out. Tell us immediately if she does, will you?"

"Of course."

"And warn Faith. I mean, tell her. What we're doing."

"I can't do that," I said, and I told them why, told them that the woman who was scheduled to deliver Faith's baby wouldn't even learn the patient's whereabouts until the last minute. I promised to tell Rogers and try to get him to deliver the message.

Then I changed the subject. "Let me ask you a brutal question."

Robert smiled. "I like an honest man."

"Is part of the reason you're doing this that you think your mother gave Louis that package to deliver?"

Peter was almost indignant. "No!" he said. Robert started to shake his head, then he clenched up tight, as though he'd been handed a live wire. He clutched at his chest and reached for his pocket. I ran to help him; Barbara, having spotted it before it happened, was at his side already.

Robert looked more irritated than in pain, like a man at the end of a long race, puffing and wheezing and holding a stitch in his side, angry at himself for not being in better shape. He waved Barbara off. "It's all right," he groaned. "It's nothing."

He was already reaching into his pocket for his medicine. He seemed to be in much better shape than last time, when the policeman had had to break the ampoule for him. This time, he did it deftly, one-handed. I heard the little crunch as the glass tube broke, and the sniff as he took a deep breath. Barbara was nodding in approval. I thought I saw a hint of relief in her expression.

As it had last time, Robert's head shot back as the fumes reached up into his head. After that, everything was different.

His head didn't come forward again—it thrashed against the back of the chair. Briefly, less than a second. Then Robert's whole body pitched forward, and he lay in a semi-fetal position on my nice blue rug, twitched a few times, then lay still.

CHAPTER TWENTY-FIVE

Peter stood by the window, screaming. You'd think his brother's condition was coming to him just now as a big surprise. I told him to shut up, but he kept on screaming. I screamed back. He shut up, then stared at me, disappointed in me for losing my head in a crisis.

I didn't care what he thought of me at the moment—whatever it was it couldn't have been anything worse than what I was thinking of myself. What the hell did I think I was doing? What had I thought I was doing when I got *into* this? All right, Faith was a friend of the family, but her problems were *none of my business*.

But I had been lonely, and bored doing my little TV listings, so I got involved. And I got my sister involved, and my mother involved, and nearly gotten them (and myself) killed. I had tried to deal with kinds of people I had no experience in nor aptitude for dealing with. I had watched a man get blown to bits, and I still wasn't sure why. I had (indirectly) cost a young cop a fractured skull. I had gone to bed with another man's wife.

I wondered how much that last incident had had to do with Robert Letron's collapse, how much it had contributed to his lying still on my carpet at that moment. I still wonder.

I told Peter to call 911 and get an ambulance. I had to repeat it before he gave the first clue he knew what I was talking about. He walked two steps toward the phone.

"We're wasting time," Barbara said. The professional tiger was back on the case. She had Robert stretched out flat on the floor, and had straddled his body about level with his navel. Her skirt had ridden well up, showing most of her legs, and I became almost absently aware that I had been wanting to see most (or all) of her legs since I'd first met her.

Not now, though, and not like this. "CPR?" I asked.

She nodded. "You know how?" I said I did, but she hardly listened to me. She looked back over her shoulder to see Peter still standing around with his hands stretching his face into a rough approximation of a basset hound.

"Get on the phone, damn you!" she hollered. Peter picked up the phone, hit buttons with a weak finger.

We got to work. Barbara began pressing down with all her weight on Robert's sternum. Sets of five. She gave a soft little grunt of effort with each compression—"uh uh uh uh uh"— pause. Over and over. That sort of noise was something else I realized I had wanted to experience with her.

This, I decided, was my punishment for taking Lucille to bed, this mockery of eroticism with a woman I truly cared about, performed over the body of Lucille's husband.

And now I had to kiss him.

I tilted Robert's head back to straighten his windpipe. I reached into his mouth to pull his tongue out of the way, then pinched his nose, and pressed my mouth over his and breathed softly into him. I took my mouth away and listened. Nothing. There was a chemical smell around him from the popper he'd used, but it soon evaporated. It was hard to get a good seal, with Robert's moustache and beard against my lips, but I pressed hard, and kept trying.

Peter had summoned an ambulance. He hung up the phone, and began hovering around us as we worked on his brother, bending, kneeling, making noises in his throat. He was like a neurotic art teacher, critical of what we were doing, but awed by the spectacle of it.

Finally, Barbara left off grunting long enough to tell him to get out of the way, to go sit down somewhere. He complied, and I was delighted. If he had knelt beside me and whimpered in my ear one more time, I would have completed a clean sweep of the Letron brothers.

In CPR training, one point they press home is to *stay at it*—

don't stop until the ambulance comes. It took several eternities (or sixteen minutes by the official New York City log) for the ambulance to get there. About halfway through the waiting time, I started to feel dizzy and sick. I started to panic. How could I breathe for Robert when I had no breath for myself?

I was *not* going to get hysterical. Not while Robert's life (possibly) depended on it. And not in front of Barbara. I suggested we switch positions, a maneuver we accomplished without missing a beat. I took deep breaths as I pressed on Robert's chest, and I soon felt better. A little. There was no visible improvement in Robert.

The ambulance men finally came. Peter had enough presence of mind to let them in. They pushed Barbara and me out of the way. I was glad to go. Barbara, an M.D., and therefore the ranking medical person on the scene, stayed close by and supervised.

She didn't have to say much—the paramedics did all the right things. They replaced secondhand air from a human lung with fresh air pumped from a black-rubber squeeze bag. They injected something into Robert's chest. They smeared two metal disks with white paste, and jolted his body with electricity. His body jumped with the shock. They did it five times.

Then they gave up.

I said a rude word. Barbara made a face and a sad shrug. Again, very professional, though I doubted she was too used to losing patients. At least I hoped she wasn't. Peter sat in his chair, looking deader than his brother.

Well, not really. Robert's skin was tinged with blue, and his arms and legs were in positions that were too uncomfortable for natural sleep. But at least there was an *expression* on his face, pained and hopeless as it may have been. Peter's face looked as though it belonged to something the shamus had already removed from the premises and brought to the undertaker, and the undertaker had used all his skill on it, it shouldn't frighten the children. It occurred to me that Robert was lying on the rug exactly where I stretched out sometimes to watch TV. I wondered if I could afford a new rug.

We had to have the medical examiner in on this, it seemed. If Barbara had been Robert's regular doctor (unlikely, for an obstetrician), she could have signed a death certificate, and that would have been it. Since she wasn't, there was going to be an autopsy. The ambulance men used the phone to call it in.

And since there was going to be an autopsy, there had to be cops, to stand guard over my living room and see that I didn't mess around with the evidence.

I had known there were going to be cops, regardless of what New York State law had to say about death and dead bodies. Anybody involved in a mess like this was going to be the subject of rigorous examination if he suddenly keeled over and died. I could have waited for things to go through channels, but I thought, why waste time?

As soon as the ambulance man was done, I asked for the phone.

"Going to call your lawyer?" he asked.

"Why?" I asked. "Do you know somebody?"

"I meet a lot of people," he said.

"Makes more sense to have a spy on the ambulance than it does to chase them in person, I suppose," I told him. He was offended and stopped talking to me. Barbara gave out with a giggle that was the first indication of nervousness I'd ever seen from her.

I called police headquarters and told them to put me in touch with Craig Rogers.

CHAPTER TWENTY-SIX

It could have been heredity, or it could have been environ-
ment. All I know is that for the first time in my life, I found
myself wanting to do something I had been making fun of my
mother about for years—clean the house in a time of stress.

It was maddening that I couldn't really do it. For one thing, I
had done a pretty good job on the place before I left for Scarsdale (that had been a pretty stressful time, too, come to think of
it), and for another, the cop wouldn't let me do a proper job.

I did the obvious stuff first—gathered up newspapers, things
like that. Then I went looking around for more to do. The place
could stand to be dusted, I thought, but that was too elaborate a
chore to start with company present.

Then I saw something on the floor I could pick up, one small,
white object about three feet away from the body. I bent over
and got my fingers around it.

"Don't touch that," the cop said. He was a mustachioed
young Hispanic with a charming smile. "It might be evidence."

"Evidence of what?" Barbara demanded. "The man had a
heart condition. We saw him collapse."

"I am sorry, ma'am." He sounded like he meant it. This guy
was going to be chief of patrol some day, maybe commissioner,
and it wouldn't do to offend too many citizens. "I'm sure you're
right," he went on. "But they told me to wait here until Lieutenant Rogers arrives. I understand you folks have met him. I
haven't, but I've heard of him, and I think it'd be best if we let
him make the decisions on what's evidence and what's not."

He had a point. I let go of the thing. Gladly, now that the feel
of dry gauze over broken glass had told me what it was—the
ampoule that had failed to save Robert's life.

Rogers arrived a few minutes later. He was not announced over the intercom. He was not alone, though he wasn't accompanied by the invasion force that had descended on my mother's house the other day. He waved his arms like a third-base coach, and men (and one woman) got busy taking pictures and making a body outline. They did it with white tape, rather than with chalk. I appreciated their concern for the welfare of my carpet, but I would just as soon they used liquid enamel and ruined the thing completely. The way it was, the decision on keeping the carpet or getting rid of it resided solely between me and my stomach.

Rogers looked around, making sure everyone was doing the right thing. Only then did he speak. First to Peter. "Mr. Letron, let me express my deepest sympathies. I know this must be a nightmare for you. Still, I will be asking some questions—I hope you understand." Peter nodded. At least his head went up and down a half inch or so. The expression on his face still might have been an oil painting.

Rogers turned to Barbara. "Dr. Metzenbaum," he said respectfully. "Lieutenant," she replied. As long as Faith's whereabouts remained a mystery, she was giving away nothing.

Then he turned to me. "Ross," he said. "Nothing personal, but I have never been as sick of the face of another human being as I am of yours."

I was too tired to be offended. "Quite all right, Lieutenant," I told him. "I'm not carrying your picture in my locket, either."

He laughed at that. I wasn't recovered to the point of jollity or anything, but they had just zipped up the green rubber bag, and they were getting Robert's body *the hell out of my apartment!* and I was starting to breathe a little better.

He started asking me questions. Barbara and Peter were taken off to different rooms by subordinates. I assume we were asked the same questions: Did I know Robert was going to be here? Do I know of any reason someone would want to kill him? Do you have any reason to suspect it wasn't a heart attack? Was there someone here who left before the ambulance arrived?

What had we been talking about? Did Robert seem afraid? And
so on.

I further assume that we gave more or less the same answers.
No (Peter would say yes, he knew Robert was coming here); no,
except possibly Faith Letron, assuming she had gone nuts. But
they had her in protective custody, didn't they? No; no; getting
Alma Letron committed; and no, not afraid, just agitated.

Rogers looked pretty agitated himself. "Why did you call the
homicide squad, then?"

"Lieutenant," I said, "I don't mind your jerking me around,
but try to give me credit for a teeny amount of brains, okay?
Here was this guy—here were *two* guys, no, *four* people involved in a whole bunch of attempted murders and a bomb
blast—three, if you don't want to count Barbara . . ."

"Barbara," he said.

"Dr. Metzenbaum. Get your eyebrow down. Anyway, the
four of us are sitting around talking about a fifth, one of us keels
over and dies, and I'm supposed to believe you wouldn't be
interested? Let's not be foolish."

"All right. So use some of the brains you want me to give you
credit for. Are you trying to get the old lady locked up because
she's the one that gave Louis the bomb?"

"How would a nice old lady like that know how to make a
bomb?"

"Are you kidding?" Rogers demanded. "For thirty years this
whole gang has had free and complete access to *a cosmetics
factory.* Three of them: one in the States, one in Canada, and
one in France. I've been checking into this. Do you know what
kinds of chemicals they use in cosmetics?" He answered his own
question. "*All* kinds, from whale puke to high explosive. Nitrobenzene. Nitroglycerine. Arsenic. God knows what all. I looked
into this after Louis staged his little fireworks show—I haven't
used my goddam after-shave lotion since. Poisons, caustics, they
use everything, either as an ingredient or in processing. Or if
they don't use it anymore, they did once. Believe me, making a
bomb is the least of their worries."

I asked him if he still wanted an answer to his question. He nodded. "In that case, I don't know."

"Thanks a lot."

"However," I went on, "if Louis was going to carry a bomb for anybody, I guess his mother would be the most likely one, right? I mean, don't you do things for your mother you wouldn't do for anyone else in the world?"

"I wouldn't blow anybody up."

"We are not talking about a normal family here."

"Mr. Understatement. But if I was Louis, and I agreed to carry a bomb for Mom, I would check the timer first."

"Timer? I thought it was supposed to go off when you opened it, and that Louis had shaken it the wrong way somehow."

"Nope," Rogers said. "It was a time bomb, all right. Found pieces of the dial. It was practically a miracle Louis even made it to your apartment. If the traffic hadn't been so light that day, Louis would have been blown up in a taxicab, somewhere, we estimate, around Fifth Avenue and Sixty-ninth Street. I mean, he allowed himself, or somebody allowed him, ten minutes to get from a midtown hotel to the Upper East Side in the middle of the afternoon. I ask you."

"I would say it showed that the bomb had been set by somebody who wasn't used to getting around in New York—"

"That would be Robert," the lieutenant pointed out.

I made a face. "It would, but Robert *was* used to getting around in Paris."

"So?"

"So the traffic in Paris is worse. They park on sidewalks. They *drive* on sidewalks, and if they run you over on the sidewalk, it's your fault. They park at the corners of the curbs. The Métro is so good in Paris because travel on the roads is damn near impossible."

"Still," Rogers said. "Robert had spent the time before the bomb went off out in the country. The rest of them had been in the city—they'd know what the traffic was like."

"So that closes the case? Robert sneaked into the city from way the hell up in Litchfield County, Connecticut, built the bomb, slipped it to his brother after miscalculating the time setting, then went home in time for the Connecticut cops to find him. How'd he get back there, a rocketship? I suppose he could make fuel from some of the chemicals they make cosmetics out of. Then, of course, he drops dead here tonight in a fit of remorse."

Rogers looked at me for a few seconds. "You done?" he said.

"Sure."

"Good. I hate to see a man make an ass of himself. Your brains should tell you I have to go through the implications of everything, whether it makes you feel guilty for sleeping with a dead man's wife or not."

Ouch, I thought. I didn't have to say anything, because the detective who'd been questioning Peter poked his head out of the kitchen.

"What is it, Morano?" Rogers said.

"He wants to talk to you. Says he has to ask you something."

"All right, bring him out. Tell Pickens to send the doctor out, too, if he's through with her." Apparently he was, because a few seconds later we were all in the living room again.

Rogers told Peter to speak. The youngest Letron cleared his throat, was unhappy with the result, and cleared it again. "It's about my mother," Peter said. "Has she been told about this?"

"We have men there, but she hasn't been told yet."

"Why did you send men there?"

"To pick something up. And to protect your mother. I understand she's raising holy hell about it, too."

"She would, of course. It's going to be worse when she learns about . . . about Robert." When his face finally moved, it worked hard; he struggled to control it, though no tears came. He sniffed, then composed himself.

"Excuse me. I still haven't been able to . . . to take it all in. I think, though, that my mother might be more tractable if I were there when she heard the news. I would be willing to tell her myself, if you like."

To my surprise, Rogers took him up on it. To my further surprise, Rogers told Morano to take Peter over to the hotel, adding, "Let him tell his mother the news, but nobody leaves until I get there."

I thought, *until he gets there.* Which meant he wasn't going himself. Amazing. What was it about me or Barbara or my humble abode that could keep him here when there was someone dramatic like Alma Letron to deal with? Rogers didn't seem to be the type to let subordinates do all the exciting work. It made me wonder what he had in mind. Did he suspect *me*, for God's sake? Or, to be even more ridiculous, Barbara?

We got the answer about twenty seconds after the door closed behind Peter Letron and his police escort. The bell rang, and the door opened again, and a uniformed cop (the same one who'd guarded the used ampoule from the Mad Housekeeper) ushered a nervous-looking Lucille Letron into the room.

CHAPTER TWENTY-SEVEN

Lucille had been crying, and as soon as she got one look at me, she started again. "Oh, Harry," she sobbed. "We did this to him. He found out, and it killed him."

This kind of remark I didn't need. I felt guilty enough already, and even before I sneaked a look and confirmed it, I could *feel* a cold glare from Barbara on me. I heard myself back in the office—no girlfriend, no one having performed the functions of a girlfriend. Well, except one. And here she was.

Her saying what she did gave Rogers a whole bunch more of questions. Undoubtedly, that was why he'd brought her here in the first place, having a cop break the bad news in the elevator on the way up to my apartment. I sometimes think Allen Funt was a policeman gone wrong.

It wasn't that Lucille's remorse wasn't genuine. She sat in a chair, playing with a gold bracelet on her wrist until I thought she was going to unscrew her hand, crying real tears, and telling the lieutenant how much she'd loved her husband, how she was sorry she hadn't treated him better. Apparently she had so much guilt, she wanted to spread it around a little.

I was willing to carry my share (and I would; I still do), but not now. I sat there trying to look repentant and innocent and misunderstood while Barbara looked at me like a microscope slide.

I had some sympathy to spare for Lucille, too, especially for little Lucille Berkowitz, hidden away in that apartment. She'd built a whole life around deceiving her husband, and not only had he never been deceived, he was now dead. I mean, even a Hostess Twinkie has *something* at the center.

Further speculation on the topic was forestalled by the doorbell. Who now? I thought. My mother? Barbara's old boyfriend, for whom, without even knowing his name, I was conceiving an intense dislike? *Lucille's* mother?

It was another cop. He had a carton, about a foot and a half long, a foot wide, and four or five inches deep.

"What is it, Jones?" Rogers asked.

"Morano told me to bring this to you, sir. It was in Mr. Peter Letron's car. It's addressed to Mr. Ross."

"Who found it?"

"Morano did, but Mr. Letron identified it. Said I should bring it to Mr. Ross. A gift for him, he said. Should I call the bomb squad?"

"Not yet," Rogers told him. "Let me see that." Rogers took the box in his hands, and held it loosely, weighing it. Then he held it to his ear and shook it gently. He held the thing an inch and a half away from his eyes and looked at all the seams in the wrapping. He sniffed it. He did everything but lick it to see what it tasted like.

Then he held it out to me and said, "Here, open it."

"It's supposed to be some of Peter's work in glass. Some animals."

"Yeah. Well, he sure wasn't sending me any presents. Don't you want to open it?"

"The possibility of its being a bomb has been brought up."

"It's not a bomb."

"How do you know?" I asked. Not snotty. I just wanted to know.

"Experience. Come on, you gonna embarrass me by making me call out the bomb squad on this?"

"Yeah," I said. "We don't want you to be embarrassed. Of course, if this is a bomb, and anybody here survives to tell about it, you're *really* going to look foolish."

"I'll risk it," he said.

Lucille was going to protest, and Barbara's face said she was working up to it. I had never felt so strongly about a woman before and blown everything so early in the relationship. That knowledge alone made me start to hope it was a bomb.

I skinned the paper off. It was a box of glass animals.

"That was still a foolish chance to take, Lieutenant," Barbara said.

"Experience," the lieutenant said. "Besides, on the bottom, in real small print, there was a message from Morano saying he had already checked it out."

"You sadistic son of a bitch!" I told him. "What *possible* good could that have done for your investigation?"

"Never mind. This isn't a computer game or something. We use what we've got, do the best we can, and see what happens."

Now he was seeing what happened when he asked Lucille questions about the box. While she told him she knew Peter did that sort of thing, but she had no idea he was planning to make me a present of any of it, I took the opportunity to look at the present itself.

Peter did nice work. The sculptures were all glass, but they were all different. There was a giraffe that had obviously been ground and etched, a walrus that had been stretched from a blob of molten glass, and a delicate blown swan, the glass stretched so thin it almost disappeared.

He finished with Lucille, and turned to Barbara, who had had about enough of him by now. Every once in a while, he would remind the gathering in general that he was saving me for last.

He never got around to me. The telephone rang. I started to get up, but one of the precinct cops beat me to the phone. He said uh huh, then covered the mouthpiece and asked the lieutenant if he wanted to talk to the Narwood Hospital.

And so much for police security, I thought. They had Faith at the Narwood Hospital, a small private hospital not far from Bellevue (not geographically, at least), and fairly close to Barbara's office, too. I wondered if the city was actually paying Narwood Hospital rates, or if the hospital was taking this off their income tax or something.

I also wondered about the perversity of life in general. Here's Rogers, keeping Faith's whereabouts secret from her own *doc-*

tor, and one phone call to one precinct cop who's there because he's a warm body—and he blurts it out in front of everybody.

Rogers cursed, then took the phone. He said his name, "Right," and "Yeah, she's on her way." He hung up the phone and turned to Barbara. "Come on, Doctor, it's time. Jones, take Mrs. Letron back to the hotel. She can rejoin her family, but *nothing* about the hospital."

He had his hand on the doorknob before he realized Barbara hadn't moved from her chair. "Doctor? You wanted to be told the second she went into labor? Well, this is it. Contractions ten minutes apart, they said."

"We've got time, then," Barbara said calmly, and I thought Rogers was going to start chewing his tie. If he ever makes a woman pregnant, she should probably do natural childbirth, so they can give *him* the anesthesia.

"What about my car?" Barbara demanded.

"Your *car?*"

Yes, her car. She had no intention of coming all the way back uptown to get her car when this was over with. Furthermore, she had no idea how long the labor was likely to take, and she didn't want her car towed away when alternate-side-of-the-street regulations went back into effect tomorrow morning. Mr. Ross knew where the car was. She would give Mr. Ross the keys, and he would drive the car down to the garage where she usually kept it, then meet her at the hospital, and give her the keys and the garage slip. If that was all right with Mr. Ross.

It took me a second to realize that was a question. "Oh," I said. "Yes. Perfectly all right."

Rogers by now would have agreed to assign a cop to carry the car downtown on his back, just so they could get *started.*

Jones left with Lucille, hustling her along so quickly, she didn't get a chance to remind me of how she and I together killed poor Robert. Barbara went through her purse, handed me her keys, and gave me a wink and a big smile. Suddenly the world looked a lot better.

It looked so good, in fact, that I was even in the mood for the radio when I reached Barbara's car twenty minutes or so later.

It took so long because I cleaned up the apartment a little before I left. Any good compulsion is worth following through.

Anyway, I got to the car, slipped into the seat, and was further confirmed in my speculation that Dr. Metzenbaum might indeed be the woman for me when I found the dial set to WCBS-FM. I hit the ignition, and heard the last notes of "Bad Boy" by the Jive Bombers dying away, only to be replaced by the news.

If I hadn't been busy pulling out of the parking space, I would have pushed a button, changed the station, and missed it.

"A fire at a landmark New York hotel has caused the evacuation of the building. Firefighters are battling the blaze at the Westbrook Hotel, where the alarm originated from less than thirty minutes ago. Fire Department sources say the twelfth and fourteenth floors are burning, and that the fire may spread. No injuries have been reported as yet. Spokesmen refused to comment on the possibility of arson. In the Middle East today—"

I reached out and clicked the thing off. To hell with the Middle East today. I pulled out onto Second Avenue. Traffic was light, and the avenue was one-way in the right direction. Rogers had to know about this. I made that little French car *move*.

CHAPTER TWENTY-EIGHT

Two hours later, I sat in the waiting room of the maternity ward of Narwood Hospital, looking gloomily at Lieutenant Rogers and feeling like an idiot.

I had made it to the hospital in record time. I had driven without the slightest regard for my life or the lives of others, almost as recklessly as a New York City cabdriver. I had even tried to attract police attention, so that they could risk *their* lives to bring the news, but without success. The cops were undoubtedly all over at the Westbrook, keeping rubberneckers out of the Fire Department's way.

When I got to the hospital, I pretended I was in Paris and parked Barbara's car half up on the sidewalk, dashed inside, talked my way past the cop at the door (he had instructions to let in the guy with the parking slip), confronted Rogers and told him the big news.

"Thanks, Ross," he said calmly.

"But this means they're probably running around loose. Peter had a propane torch up there—he used it to make his glass stuff. That's probably how the fire started."

"Ross, I've thought of all this already. And they *are* running around loose."

"How do you know that?"

"They put radios in police cars these days."

"Oh," I said. After that, I decided to give my brain a brief rest, like for the remainder of the 1980s. Radios in police cars. What would they think of next?

Rogers, not knowing that I had switched off, went on talking. "I heard from Morano right after the fire started. There was a panic in the building, and my guys got things straightened out.

The old lady disappeared; Peter is gone, too—Morano thinks he's out looking for his mother. Lucille turned up again, bringing the news that she let slip the name of the hospital."

"That's why the guard at the door," I said.

"Right. Not that it will do much good, really. There are a lot of ways in and out of here, and I don't have the men to cover them all." He sighed. "Anyway, your doctor friend promises me it will all be over pretty soon. Once the baby's born, the game is up, right?"

"That's the theory," I told him. "We're dealing with crazy people here, remember."

"Catch me forgetting," he said.

So we went to the waiting room. It was a dingy, depressing place. The magazines were ancient. Rogers said, "What the hell is this? For the kind of money this hospital charges—"

"Nobody uses the waiting room anymore," I told him. "All the expectant fathers are in with their wives, holding their hands and telling them how to breathe."

Rogers turned a washy sea-green. "Jesus," he said reverently. "And yet, sex is so much *fun* at first."

That was the end of conversation for a couple of hours. I read about Watergate in old magazines, watching Rogers as he lifted his head like clockwork every twenty-five seconds to look at the door to the delivery room.

At last he said, "Ross, you got something serious going with the doctor?"

"Is this relevant to the investigation?"

"To hell with the investigation for a second. Man to man. Humor me."

I looked for trickery in his face, couldn't find any, and decided to take a chance. "I'm working on it. Why?"

"I thought so. I've done all I could for you. Don't blow it."

"All you could? The way you had Lucille Letron show up? I suppose that *was* all you could do, short of having her waltz in there naked and shoot me."

"You don't know what you're talking about," he informed me.

"I'm your best friend, Ross. You screwed Lucille. There was nothing to that but getting your rocks off, right?"

"Right," I said. I wondered if a homicide lieutenant had ever been punched out in a maternity ward waiting room before. "I'm having it engraved on my tombstone—'He Screwed Her, But Only To Get Off His Rocks.'"

"Okay, but now you don't have to go through your life worrying if the doctor is going to find out, do you? Once I saw how it was going down, I saved your ass. I treated you like a turd, and she got all motherly and forgave you. Insisted you drive her car down. Winked at you when she thought I couldn't see. Your slate is clean; what happens now is up to you. Don't blow it, that's all."

I looked at him. This, I decided, is a man you could never get to the bottom of—he's never doing what you think he's doing.

"Why?" I said. "Why go to all that trouble?"

He shrugged. "No trouble," he said. "Besides, I know what it's like. There's a woman I let get away. She's married to a guy—a great guy—but there's no way that marriage should work. It just does. And I see her all the time, and it eats at me. I look at you, I see a guy who'd be flat-out *killed* by something like that, so I thought I'd do the best I could for you."

I was still taking all that in when Barbara poked her strawberry-blond head through the door and said, "It's a girl. Seven pounds, seven ounces. I wanted her to name her 'Lucky,' but Faith insists on Paula Harriet."

I've never smoked in my life, but at that moment, I wanted a cigar. Rogers was beaming. Barbara was laughing at us. Let her.

"Harry, she wants to see you," Barbara said.

"The baby wants to see me?"

"No, idiot. *Faith* wants to see you."

"You're sure it's all right, now."

"Who's the doctor around here? Of course it's all right." She came and took me by the hand and led me into the inner precincts.

Faith hardly made a bulge under the blankets. Looking at her face, you could see why they called it "labor." She looked like she'd just run a marathon. And won.

"Harry," she said. "Harry, she's beautiful."

"I knew we'd see you through," I said. It was a lie. There were a lot of times when I doubted it sincerely.

"And you did. It's over, Harry. Little Paula and I can live in peace."

I sure hoped so. "Peace?" I said. "You have obviously never lived in the same house with a baby." She laughed. "Seriously, Faith, if she's half as pretty and half as brave as her mother, she's going to be one hell of a kid."

"She will be," Faith said. "She's Paul's child, too."

"Can I tell my mother the good news?"

"Oh yes! My God, I forgot. And Sue, too." Her face got grim. "And tell the family. I want them to know."

"Right," I said.

Her joy was too big to be kept out for long, and she started bubbling again.

"Harry, go look at the baby. She's *beautiful.*"

"Yes, Harry," Barbara said. "Go look at the baby. Her mother is exhausted, and is going to take a nap."

I went to tell Rogers I was going to look at the baby, and he decided he'd come along, too.

"Hell," he said. "I waited long enough for it to get born."

"For *her* to get born," I corrected.

We walked down to the end of the hallway where there was a large plate-glass window with babies behind it like items offered for sale. I pushed an intercom button and said "Letron" to a masked nurse. She held up a squirming something that was moist and red where head and hands stuck out of a garment that was basically a pink cloth sack. She had a full head of black hair, and opened her mouth in a yawn, revealing toothless gums.

"My God," Rogers said.

"That is a perfectly good baby," I told him. "They all look like this when they're born. The bald ones look worse. I think she's a darling, myself."

"My God," Rogers said again.

"And," I went on, "you should keep this in mind: this is undoubtedly the wealthiest baby born in the world today. Just by being born, she becomes the major owner of a giant corporation. A birthday gift from her father."

"Yeah," Rogers said, "but what I still want to know is—"

I never found out what he still wanted to know. There was a noise from the end of the corridor, something halfway between a scream and a roar. I turned, and saw that the noise was coming from Mrs. Alma Letron. Somehow, I wasn't surprised to see her. She was kind enough to repeat her yell over and over, so we could make out the words.

"She won't get away with it! She won't get away with it!"

She started running down the corridor at us, waving her right arm over her head. She had something in her hand; when she ran under one of the lighting fixtures, I could see it was a great big claw hammer.

Let the cops handle this, I thought, just before she put a move on Rogers and ran around him like he was a fire hydrant. The Giants should have a halfback with moves like that.

Harry, I told myself, it is up to you. Of all people. How about that.

By now, she wasn't even looking at me. For her, two things existed in the world—that sheet of glass, and her hammer. No, three. The baby behind that sheet of glass. The ironic thing was that the nurse had already taken off with Faith's baby still in her arms. God knew what Alma intended, but I didn't think it would be especially healthy for the five or six other people's kids behind that window.

I got way over to the left side of the corridor to cut off her room to maneuver. Then, when she tried to go around me to my right, I dived at her, wrapped my arms around her waist, and brought her down with a tackle that would have made my old coach proud.

Then she started hitting me with the hammer. I guess she figured she'd carried the goddam thing this far, she was damn well going to use it.

I could feel things crunching in my body under the blows, but

I didn't feel any pain. Yet. Next time I did this, I would make it a point to pin her arms.

It seemed to be taking forever for Rogers to come to my aid. I looked up to see where he was, and the hammer came down on my nose, and that was the end of Sunday as far as I was concerned.

CHAPTER TWENTY-NINE

I woke up and said, "Stupid."

I wondered why I said it, but only for a second. Bewilderment was rapidly replaced by concern over my vision—the world I could see was a narrow, rough-edged rectangle surrounded by blackness, like a sloppy CinemaScope screen.

"You are not stupid," a woman with a Jamaican accent said. "You are a 'ero. And you are making medical 'istory."

My voice cracked. "Medical history? What's the matter with me?" I turned to look at the owner of the voice, a plump happy black woman in a nurse's uniform. It was a mistake. I no longer saw a rectangle, I saw stars.

"Take it easy, mon," she said. "You'll 'eal, in time. You got a broken nose and some cracked ribs."

That explained the vision problems—I was looking through mounds of swollen eye-socket flesh surrounded by bandages. It was a wonder I could see anything at all. Gently, I raised a hand and confirmed the rest. "Where does the medical history come in?"

She laughed. "You are the first mon ever to 'ave 'is nose looked after by an obstetrician. She was sitting by you all night. She got a big plastic surgeon to get out of bed, and 'e came and fixed you up all pretty."

"Is she still here?"

She laughed again and nodded. "I go tell 'er you are awake."

Ten seconds later, Barbara came in, and we shared Our First Kiss, a little peck on the square millimeter of my lip the bandages left exposed.

"How are you?" she said.

"I feel as if someone has shoved a flat rock up under my upper lip into my forehead."

"That'll happen," she assured me.

"It certainly will," I agreed. "Thanks for getting your friend up here for me."

"Don't mention it," she said. "Protecting my investment."

"What have I missed? What day is it?"

"It's only Monday." She looked at her watch. "About two o'clock in the afternoon. Your rescue of the window and the babies was the high point of the action," she assured me. "Do you have Blue Cross?"

I tried to nod, decided that was a bad idea, said yes instead. Then she gave me the wrap-up.

There was a regular little convention at the hospital. I was here. A couple of doors down was the policeman Alma had belted in the head to gain access to the maternity ward in the first place. Faith and Paula were still in the maternity ward, safe and sound, and under twice as much protection, even though they were completely safe now.

I wondered how I knew that.

Alma was under restraint in the psycho ward. Peter, who had turned up at a police station about 2 A.M., saying he had despaired of finding his mother, and that he was afraid she was going to do something terrible, was haunting the waiting room up there. Lucille was with him. If I remembered the financial deals correctly, with Paul's estate being distributed with the birth of his daughter, Lucille would get all the money she and Robert had before the baby was born, a fortune to me, but chicken feed compared to the money Faith now controlled on behalf of her daughter. The big surprise winner were Alma Letron and her surviving son, who would split the money Paul had put aside for the four of them. This had not been chicken feed when it had been a four-way split; now it would be fairly monumental.

Now I thought I knew why I'd said "stupid" when I woke up. The whole thing had been so *pointless*. Only a perverted, maniacal family pride could have found a purpose to kill Faith or the baby in the first place. And the attempts themselves had been so *inefficient*. Pushing her down in the street, trying to run her over with a car. Trying to run a car with her in it off the road, if that little incident in Westchester had been in fact one of the attempts. So chancy. So likely to fail. Hell, they *did* fail.

I may have wanted to kill people in the past (old girlfriends, editors at The Grayness), but I never felt that way strongly enough or long enough to actually get around to *planning* it. But even such a gentle soul as myself could see that if you really wanted somebody dead, you should either get him (or her) alone and shoot, stab or strangle them, or spend the money on a professional to get it done right.

I mean, let's face it. When *I* can save somebody from a murder attempt, she must not have been in much danger in the first place. You'd almost think . . .

Why almost? What if you went ahead and just *thought* it?

"Not stupid," I said.

Barbara said, "What?"

"It wasn't stupid," I told her. "It was crazy, and bizarre, and more than a little nasty, but it wasn't stupid. It all *makes sense*. Not *perfect* sense, mind you, but sense nonetheless."

She bent to kiss me again, this time on the forehead.

"No," I told her, "I am not delirious. I've got to talk to Rogers."

"Why?" she demanded. "It's over, Harry. Get well, will you? I'm not going to get involved with a man who won't let go of trouble, even when it's over."

"When it's over," I told her solemnly, "I'll let go."

"Oh," she said. She was no longer bantering. "It's like that."

"Yeah," I said. "It's like that. Get Rogers here as soon as he can make it, okay?"

CHAPTER THIRTY

By four o'clock that afternoon, I was sitting in a wheelchair, en route to the psycho ward of Narwood Hospital. I was just visiting, not being committed. If anyone deserved to become a student at the Happy Academy, it was Detective Lieutenant Craig Rogers, N.Y.P.D.

As usual, he was full of surprises. When I told him everything I had in mind, he'd stroked his chin and said, "Sure, I thought of that last night, as soon as I heard about the fire."

"You did, huh? Have you done anything about it yet?"

"Don't get so snotty, Ross—with a broken nose, you can't afford it."

Barbara told him not to be disgusting.

Rogers ignored her. "I'm a police officer, Ross. An officer of the *law*. I took an oath to uphold the law, and I'm stuck with it. I can be—and have been—sure enough to stake my mother's life that somebody's guilty, but if I don't come up with enough evidence to convince a jury, he hasn't done anything."

"There's got to be *some* evidence," I said. The rock under my face was starting to throb.

"Where do you think I've been all day, on no sleep? I've been kicking ass all over town trying to find some evidence. So far, not a goddam bit."

"So what are you going to do?"

"Keep looking until the brass makes me quit. Then I quit."

"And the killer walks."

"You've got a mad on about this particular killer, don't you?"

"What do you think?"

"I think this is something beyond, shall we say, an abstract love of justice. Something personal."

"That was my mother and my sister in the car with me and Faith, Rogers. And my sister and me just outside when the bomb went off. Accident or not, we were around."

"I don't believe any of this," Barbara said.

"Doctor," he said, "believe it. The question is whether Ross here would do something about it, if he had the chance."

"You know I would."

Rogers smiled. "I'm glad you said that," he told me.

So here I was, not a cop, not even a crime reporter. Not even a goddam *process server,* for God's sake. Here I was, with every bit of my no-experience dealing with dangerous, cornered psychopaths behind me, going to try to pull a magic trick on a murderer. No. Trying to get the murderer to pull a reflexive magic trick, and have the evidence appear by the killer's own act.

Not that it was a bad plan. It was a good plan, and I knew all the reasons Rogers couldn't do it himself. He was a cop, and everybody knew he was a cop. People would be on guard around him. I was just Harry Ross, someone the killer had played by the numbers, like an Emenee organ. When I lit off a firework, people would jump.

That was the theory.

We found Lucille and Peter sitting around outside the guarded entrance to the psychiatric care wing. They were doing a pretty good impression of Rogers and me, but they came to life when I spoke to them. They were all concern and apologies. Peter assured me that I need have no worries about medical expenses. Faith had already made the same promise; the plastic surgeon was charging me practically nothing as a professional courtesy to Barbara; and I had insurance. All my problems should be as well taken care of as my bill at Narwood Hospital.

"How's Faith?" Lucille asked. I told her she was fine. Then I looked at her and waited. "And the baby?" she said at last. Barbara said in her experience, she had never seen a better baby. Lucille's nose wrinkled for a split second. I didn't know exactly what her hang-up was, but I wanted to get out of the wheelchair, grab Lucille by the hair, and drag her down to look at little Paula and the rest of them, and defy her to tell me the difference between a "natural" child and the "experiment."

"Have you been talking to Lieutenant Rogers?" Peter asked. "Do you think he'll go along if we have Mother privately committed?"

That was beautiful—I couldn't have asked for a better straight line. "I don't know. I guess it would depend on the medical consensus. What do you think, Barbara?"

She picked right up on it. "I don't know. Mental health isn't really my field, but it was my patient she was after, so I'm sure my opinion would be asked . . ."

"Yes?" Peter asked. "What would you say?" Lucille wanted to know.

Barbara bit her lip, pondering it. "I don't really . . . Listen, I've got to do something inside, come with me and we'll still talk."

Lucille was puzzled. "Inside the psychiatric ward? I thought mental health wasn't your field."

"It's not, Mrs. Letron. But disturbed women get pregnant, and pregnant women get disturbed."

So we went inside. Barbara kept talking without actually saying anything until we reached the nurses' section. Then she said, "Excuse me," went behind the desk, and started looking at charts. She held the clipboard in her left hand; only I noticed what she was doing with her right.

I raised my hand and indicated my bandages. "Too bad you weren't around in time to save me from *this*," I said to Peter.

He looked at me for a second, decided it was a joke and that an injured man could be forgiven a lapse of taste, and laughed.

"Of course," I went on, "it must be harder to figure out how long after you've primed her your mother is going to go off than it is a bomb."

"What are you talking about?" Lucille demanded.

"Look at him, Lucille," I said, keeping my eyes on Peter. "He knows what I'm talking about. He knows he killed his brothers. Louis, with the bomb, your husband wi—"

"Robert had a heart attack!" she protested. Peter's smile said, "Answer that one."

"He had an *angina* attack. People live for years with angina. How many weeks went by without your husband having them? And more importantly, how much did they hamper his having a normal life?"

"He . . . it . . . didn't hamper him. As long as he kept taking his medicine—"

"Remember you said that, Lucille." I turned to her brother-in-law. "I know you did it, Peter. I'm pretty sure how, and I bet I even know why."

"I saved your life, Ross," the young man reminded me.

"Yeah. I appreciate that less now that I know you were the one who put it in danger in the first place. What did you do? Did you tell him it was glass animals? You gave Louis the package and sent him on his merry way, right? Then you followed him, to make sure the bomb went off, or to intercept the package if for some reason it didn't.

"But your timing got messed up by the light traffic. You couldn't have foreseen it, but suddenly it was imperative to keep that bomb away from me. Especially away from Faith. So you had to show yourself. It worked out pretty well for you; Louis was gone, and you were a hero to Faith and her friends. You couldn't be the one trying to kill her; didn't you save her life?"

"It still sounds good to me," he said.

"You're crazy," Lucille said.

"Let *him* call me crazy." I didn't take my eyes off Peter. He didn't stop smiling.

"Go on," he said.

"Oh, you weren't about to stop me."

"You still have to explain why I saved Faith's life if I was trying to kill her."

"That's the whole point, Peter. That was the whole brilliance and sickness of your plan. You weren't."

"He wasn't?" Lucille demanded. "He wasn't *what?*"

"Trying to kill Faith."

I was beginning to think it was a mistake to have Lucille for an audience while I tried to do this. She was coming up with all the histrionic reactions I'd been hoping to get from Peter. All he had to do was stand there and smile, while Lucille got wilder and wilder.

She was practically screaming by now. "Then who *was* trying to kill her?"

"Nobody," I explained. "I mean, Peter made the attacks, didn't you, Peter? Look at how he keeps smiling, Lucille. Haven't I said enough to piss him off yet? *You're* practically hysterical, and I haven't accused you of a damn thing."

"You've had a blow on the head," Peter said calmly. "I'm making allowances. Or I'm giving you enough rope to hang yourself. I haven't decided yet."

"Well," I said, "I'll just keep talking until you do. Barbara, how are you coming with that?"

"Just fine," she said.

"Good, good, then we'll be able to wind this up soon. Lucille, Peter didn't have any great regard for Faith's well-being, or the baby's either. But he didn't want to kill her. He couldn't kill her, not and go through with his plan. Because if he killed her, the investigation would come down on your family like the proverbial ton of bricks. The motive screamed out. Faith went around screaming it out, and so did your mother-in-law. It might have been your mother-in-law's ravings about the family fortune and all that, that gave him the idea."

I waited for somebody to say "What idea?" but nobody did. I went on unprompted. "What Peter wanted to do," I said, "and what he has damn near succeeded in doing, was to use Faith as a smokescreen, allowing him to kill his brothers and frame his mother for the crime.

"You will notice," I said, "that he didn't really do anything *lethal* until he sent that bomb. That was after Faith came to me. What difference did I make? I had used the resources of The Greatest Newspaper In The World to look into the situation. I knew how much of Faith's story was true. When the shit started to go down, I gave Faith a credibility with the cops she never had when she went to them on her own.

"So now that Louis was dead, it looked like he was the one behind the threats on Faith's life, Peter was a hero. Why didn't he stop? Why didn't you stop, Peter?"

"Why don't you stop, Ross? This is getting tiresome."

I ignored him. "You didn't stop because you still had Robert to take care of. Killing Robert was even simpler and nastier than killing Louis had been. You have access to poisonous chemicals; you work with glass. It would be a simple matter for you to, say, empty one of Robert's ampoules, replace the medicine with what? Cyanide? Nitrobenzene? Something deadly that worked fast and evaporated. Then seal it up again. They're going to look for it during the autopsy, now. They probably wouldn't have before."

Peter shrank. Not a lot, and not for long, but the news about the autopsy stung him.

"That used ampoule I found on the floor, the one the cop wouldn't let me finish picking up—it was bone dry, and it shouldn't have been. It should have felt oily, Barbara tells me. You switched it while you were hanging around, getting in our way while we were doing CPR. After you dawdled in calling the ambulance, just in case we might pull off a miracle and save him. I don't know when you planted the poison ampoule on your brother; I don't suppose it matters. You didn't plan on a doctor's being present when he snapped the thing; I remember you were less than gracious about Barbara's coming upstairs. In the end, I guess you decided it didn't matter. Sometime soon, Robert would have an angina attack, and he would reach for the medicine, and he would get the poison, and he would die. Everybody would take it for a heart attack. It just had to happen *before* Faith had the baby."

"Why?" Lucille demanded.

"Because Paul set things up so that his estate was distributed not when he died, but *when the baby was born*. If Robert was alive when that happened, he would come into his share; if he died after that, his money would go to you."

I studied Peter. I wished I had a monocle or something to look at him through.

"You know," I said, "I really wish I knew how much of this you planned. Did you know how close Faith was to having the baby? I mean, you just got Robert killed under the wire. How many phony ampoules did you gimmick up? I bet you fixed it so they were *all* poison. Did you work on your mother some more? Are you the one who's been stoking her hatred of Faith from the beginning?"

No answer but a smile. But I could see sweat on his forehead. Somewhere in the universe, there existed a bunch of booby-trapped ampoules. Peter had been in the hospital all night; he hadn't had a chance to destroy them.

"How sure were you that you wouldn't kill yourself or Faith during the car chase you set up? Hanging around, clubbing a cop, stealing a police car—that was a lot of risk to go through just to keep the idea of Faith's danger alive. But then, I guess you had to. You had to have the attention. I'm sure you like it. And you had to keep people thinking in terms of a threat to Faith. It didn't much matter what they thought, as long as it kept their minds off the fact that you, by killing your brothers, had doubled your share of Paul's money.

"And then tonight, you brought things to a close. You used the news of Robert's death—news you had gone out of your way to get permission to give her—to drive your mother over the edge. What did you tell her? That Faith had killed Louis and Robert? It didn't matter. Lucille let slip where they were, you set the hotel on fire with your little torch. You gave the poor, sick, old woman a hammer, helped her get away during the confusion, then disappeared for a couple of hours.

"And now," I said, "it's a clean sweep. Your mother is off the rails; you have every expectation of being appointed conservator. That means, between what you get in your own right, and what you control of your mother's, you've got the whole thing. Four times the money you would have gotten in the first place.

"But there's more, Peter, isn't there. I haven't known your family all that long, thank God, but it seems to me nobody ever took you too seriously. Paul had business genius; Robert had responsibility; Louis had charm. And women. You had glass animals. You were the baby. Never got any respect."

"Do you expect this childish bullshit to make me confess, Ross?"

We'd been hoping for it. "Of course not," I said.

"Well, here's a get-well present. Better than glass animals. I did it."

I thought Lucille was going to faint. "In front of witnesses," she said.

"Some witnesses," Peter said. "A man with an ax to grind against my family, and two women he sleeps with."

Barbara blushed. I could hardly believe it. I thought of correcting him, since Barbara and I had *not* slept together. That, however, was a situation I planned to rectify as soon as practicable, so I let it go.

I corrected him about something else. "Not just us," I said. He begged my pardon.

"You've been talking to more than just the three of us. You see, Dr. Metzenbaum opened the intercom from the nurses' station to one of the rooms on this floor right after she went behind the counter. So other people have been listening."

"Like Lieutenant Rogers," Lucille said. "My God, he killed Robert. He killed Robert." She said it all on one note. It was like being at a séance.

"Like Lieutenant Rogers," I echoed. "Heard enough, Lieutenant?"

Rogers's voice came from down the hall. "Plenty. Don't try to go anywhere, Mr. Letron, all the exits are guarded."

There was never a more unnecessary warning. Peter was paralyzed.

I spun my wheelchair around. "Here he comes now. There's an audio technician with him, and a man who came up from downtown with a court order. And Peter?"

He turned to look at me.

"Peter, guess whose room they set up in?"

"No," he said. "No."

Alma Letron came out of her room and walked rapidly toward us. She went right around the cops, making Rogers 0-for-2 at stopping her, but somehow I don't think he was trying too hard.

She walked up to her son and put her hands on his shoulders. "I never wanted to have you," she said. "You were a mistake."

Then she spat in his face.

CHAPTER THIRTY-ONE

The cops found the ampoules; they had Peter's fingerprints all over them, and the autopsy showed the same chemical in them and in Robert's system. Peter wasn't as brilliant as I thought—the way he ran things, the minute somebody suspected him, he was through. I guess they took that as proof of insanity, because he never stood trial. He was committed. His mother was committed. Lucille wound up controlling all the money. I hope it makes her happy.

My mother is dating Hi Marks, at last. I think I'm going to get the opportunity to give my mother away in a much nicer fashion than Peter Letron tried with his.

Sue has moved out of the dorm at Syracuse, and taken a house with Faith, The World's Richest Infant, and a nurse. Faith is studying chemistry and business at SU. The idea is, if she's going to hand over a cosmetics firm in good shape to the new owner, she'd better know something about it.

Barbara is now renting out the condo in Fort Lee and living in Manhattan with me. We'll get married as soon as business lightens up a little. Bumper crop of Yuppie babies this year. Every man should sleep with a gynecologist (not this one). Not only do they know exactly what they want you to do, they know *why*.

I was not allowed to write up the Letron story for The Grayness. I was, however, the source of about a million stories, and I finally got to do a first person feature for the Sunday magazine. That led to a few others, and I now work for the magazine exclusively.

I am a very happy guy, these days. Sometimes I wonder if I should feel guilty about owing all the best things in my life to such a mess of fear and murder.

Then I think, to hell with it. I didn't ask for it to happen. I did my best. I made one big mistake, but I didn't deliberately hurt anybody who didn't deserve to be hurt. I mention this to Rogers sometimes, and he tells me I'm nuts.

"You act like you're the only one who came out of this happy. Hell, I got a lot of good press over it, and everybody else came out great except the dead, the nuts and the guilty. And you couldn't have helped them, anyway."

I hope he's right, but I don't go brooding about it; I think of how glad I'm going to be when work is over and I meet Barbara.

For the first time in a long time, I've got no complaints.

About the Author

Philip De Grave is the pseudonym an award-winning American author gives to one fragment of a splintered personality. His real identity is a secret, but not so secret a true mystery fan couldn't find or figure it out. The Crime Club also published the first De Grave novel, *Unholy Moses*.